Lydia Millet was born in Boston in 1968 but was raised in Toronto, Canada. She studied at the University of North Carolina and spent some of that time in France and England. After graduating she lived in Los Angeles, where she worked as a magazine copyeditor, but when *Omnivores* was accepted for publication she moved back to North Carolina to pursue a master's degree in environmental management at Duke University. In May 1996 she moved to New York City where she is now writing full-time.

omnivores

a novel by
lydia millet

A *Virago* Book

Published by Virago Press 1998

First published in the United States in 1996
by Algonquin Books
First published in Great Britain in 1997
by Virago Press

Copyright © Lydia Millet 1996

The moral right of the author has been asserted

A CIP catalogue record for this book
is available from the British Library.

ISBN 1 86049 432 3

Typeset in Melior by M Rules
Printed and bound in Great Britain by
Clays Ltd, St Ives plc

Virago
A Division of
Little, Brown and Company (UK)
Brettenham House
Lancaster Place
London WC2E 7EN

*The author wishes to thank Aviva Goode,
Randolph Heard, Robert Odom, Timothy
Power, Memsy Price and Dorothy
Stefanski for their kind advice.*

part one

tyrannosaurus
rex

one

'Your dead bugs are delicate,' said Bill, brushing a flake
of ash off his suit sleeve. 'Grease the pin up before you
pierce 'em. Or else the little shits will fall apart.'

Home from the crematorium, he took her under his
wing. In his private gallery, in display cases lining the
walls, were legions of the dead. There were those who
crumbled in their tombs, furred bodies frail as dry leaves,
leg segments long departed from their casings. A stray
proboscis here, a palpus there. Mr. Kraft was less a hobby-
ist than a gamesman. His chief interest was the animal
world: a grandiose moth collection, and then there were
the cockfights. His new mission, he proclaimed, was to
school his daughter in the science of nature. 'Your female
tussock moth,' he advised on their first night in training,
'has no wings. Can't fly. She lives to mate.' After which,
with a chortle, he swung off in the direction of her
mother's room, the invalid's sanctum, his flat-footed feet
crunching down on a carpet of Noctuidae corpses.

He insisted that the house be clean, and hired maids
for this purpose, but his workroom, fitted out in dark
wood, was littered with the musty debris of a thousand
captures and purchases. If Estée put a drink down on a

table she was sure to find, when she reached for it later,
a dried-up bagworm floating and bobbing near the rim.
He counseled intimacy with the specimens. The moths
and butterflies, their cocoons and glistening pupae of
infancy, had to be as familiar to his daughter as her fingers and toes. He administered tests to her on every other
day. He was The Inquisition. His jiggling pounds and
florid bursting face loomed close at every turn: he was a
monstrous pachyderm, a monument in flesh who cornered her with his bulk, dogged her steps and breathed
her exhalations. 'Suborder Ditrysia?' he would bellow.
'Describe! Define!' If she was slow he leapt into the
breach. 'Females with two genital openings, you stupid
girl, receptive on eighth abdominal segment!' As
penance he made her crush a specimen in her hand —
something expendable, a common clothes moth or burrowing sod webworm. She was not allowed to wash it off
till the session was over; for each wrong answer or long
silence he would sacrifice an insect. At the start of her
apprenticeship there were times she had to clutch whole
handfuls of crushed bodies, whimpering for him to let
her go. 'You get ten wrong answers in a row, you eat
them all,' he warned. She had to chew before she swallowed. 'You keep this up, you pay the price,' he
threatened when her scholarship did not improve. He
vowed to make her ingest a goat moth, whose wingspan
was over ten inches.

Thus while other teenagers were surfing or practicing
birth control she was learning superfamilies in her room,
murmuring in the stillness of midnight, 'Zygaenoidea,
Cossoidea, *Danaus plexippus*.' Mr. Kraft claimed his

strictness was in her best interests. 'Discipline, my girl.
As my only child,' he told her sternly over a glass of
sherry, flicking his wrist to dislodge a chrysalis from the
hairs on the back of his hand, 'you're gonna hafta be
prepared.' But he forgot to say for what and dozed off in
his armchair, leaving her free to avert her eyes from the
caverns of his nostrils.

She carried food to her mother in the evening and was
trapped in a chair near the bed while the invalid prised
pistachios from their fuchsia shells, dye mottling her
fingertips, or sucked oysters down her throat, false teeth
in effervescent liquid on the bedside table. Facing the
canopied bed, whose aura was of medicine and rot, was
the shrine, mama's altar to the Bettys. Estée's mother
worshiped all famous Bettys, though there were only a
few represented here: Grable, Friedan, Crocker, Rubble,
Page, and Boop. Photographs, memorabilia, articles of
clothing or publicity redolent of Bettydom hung on a
tabernacle of gingham and lace. Betty disciplined her
daughter in stillness: if Estée fidgeted while her mother
ate, if she let her feet shuffle over the carpet in boredom, stretched out an arm in fatigue, or idly shifted in
her seat, her mother would embark on a hunger strike.
Pushing away her food she would sigh and remember
the halcyon days. 'I had all my teeth,' she would muse,
'my own hair, and it was golden like yours,' while Estée
bent over the supper tray, arranging morsels in appealing
patterns.

Her dad brought bettors home to watch the roosters. In
the skylit atrium men jeered and cheered, yelling and
pumping arms at their favorites. Afterward they gathered

with beers in the armory, bills changed hands, backslapping ensued, and Estée would linger under the dome, feathers floating up to cling to her legs, to watch the final throes of a mangled cock left behind on his battle site. He might be covered in the loops of his entrails as she knelt beside him, stroking an eyeless head as legs trembled, claws clutched, heartbeat stopped. The victory cock, corralled again in a sandy meshed pen beneath the garbled branches of a eucalyptus, strutted and crowed to lose another day.

Blundering into Betty's boudoir while his two girls were sitting quietly, Bill was prone to bluster, 'Betty, is that a smut on your nose or am I seeing double?' referring to his progeny. He would take Estée aside and say, 'Your mother named you for Lauder the cosmetics queen, so let's see you get gorgeous!' and jab his daughter in the ribs before she could reply. Estée hated her name, but Betty was proud of it and would not budge. 'So feminine,' she liked to murmur. She had been inspired by a jar of cellulite cream on her nightstand, which reminded her of shopping days long past. Mrs. Kraft's strained energies had during healthier times been channeled into volunteer work for humanitarian causes – civic beautification, Californian Ladies for the Right to Bear Arms, Orange County Citizens for Reagan. One year she'd thrown a charity dinner for hideously malformed children and financed a six-year-old's harelip surgery with the proceeds. Now, bedridden, she concentrated on the home front. On her stronger days she was a hurricane. She made Estée sit beside a bust of Betty Grable, sculpted craftily in painted Styrofoam, and

leering from her pillowed throne held up a Day-Glo hula
hoop whose plastic sting was vicious.

'Be like Betty,' she ordered through clenched teeth,
and Estée became inanimate. Over her shoulder quivered the hoop, eager to lash if she betrayed herself
through movement. Estée and the bust stared with identical blankness at the surface of the wall. She was fond of
the bust: there was safety in numbers. A stranger might
say they didn't have much in common, but she certainly
knew better. Admittedly, according to Bill's dog-eared
Gray's Anatomy, the bust was missing features Estée had,
was lacking optic nerves, the fibrous tissue of the brain,
and neither did it possess the power of autonomous
motion; but these were minor points. In space their posi-
tions were similar. A tenderness would overtake her as
she sat, and if she'd been able to she would have reached
out and touched the curve of its nose, the slant of its
Styrofoam cheekbone, the strands of its blond, Authentic
Human Hair wig.

Massage was her duty. Betty would lie prone while
Estée rubbed aromatic oils into her back, fragments of
dead skin adhering to her palms and thumbs. The household dust was human epidermal cells sloughed off by
Betty in paralysis. Her skin lined mantelpieces and old
china, goblets and chandeliers, and with a breeze or
Estée's breath would float up in clouds and resettle on
carpets and floorboards. Estée had witnessed, since a
tiny tot, the constant exfoliation of Betty. Into her Fisher-
Price tape recorder, by means of which she'd kept a
private journal since she found it in a toy closet when
she was ten, she confided, 'The skin on top is clear, you

can hold it up to the light and see through it. How does she store all those layers underneath?' Artificial talons were glued to the blackened crescent stubs of Betty's fingernails, these in a bright rainbow of colours – another task assigned to Estée in the name of filial devotion. The maids were paid to keep house, but Estée was caretaker of its doyenne. Her schedule was tight and left few hours for diversion, and her movements outside the home were monitored with rigor. On rare occasions she escaped to freedom after school hours, but Bill, who waited in the car outside school grounds with a stopwatch in hand, caught up with her and meted out due punishment. 'Told you, Esty,' he would lecture, 'nothing but weirdos out there. They let 'em walk on the streets. Criminals, reprobates, and child molesters Esty. Death can jump on you lickety-split. It's chaos Esty. At home's the only place with order. You stay put and don't stray. Sixteen years I fed you, not going to be ripped off now by some maniac with a switchblade. My investment in the future, girl. And don't cry. Where's your damn guts?'

Her father's girth was an expanding universe. His stomach ballooned, his chest became breasts, his ankles settled into tubes of wrinkly fat. He stopped short of four hundred pounds by the breadth of a hair. He felt no shame in his body's excesses, explosions, secretions, its rude assault on the innocent air. When they stood in the same room he was always within a two-foot radius of her, belching, farting, allowing himself every breach of decorum from which, during the day, he felt himself required to abstain. Massive, greedy, and abhorrent, he quizzed her on the habits of

Yponomeuta. Seating himself to defecate he would make her stand at the bathroom door and rhyme off the members of superfamily Bombycoidea.

As her apprenticeship wore on Bill got sick of the laborious process of taxonomy and passed the mantle to her. She was the one to label the specimens he imported, to pin them on pads and encase them in glass. He wanted only to stroll through the gallery, admiring the blossoming crowd of rare species. He devoted his days to the crematorium, though he had a host of other assets, because it was his favorite enterprise. On his return in the evenings he would drink, put his feet up, and watch her at her labor.

Her bedroom was subject to warrantless searches and seizures. Her father snuck in often while she slept and woke her up in the middle of the night, stark naked. 'What were you doing with this? *This?*' he would threaten, and shake in her groggy face some object he had found, burrowing in her drawers or closet, behind which she could see, since her mattress lay at the level of his crotch, purple plumlike testicles waggling and peeking from between columnar, dimpled thighs, and the poking inquisitive head of a small pink cigar.

Focus was Bill's mantra: only a small canon of possessions was allowed, related to her studies at school or at home. Foreign material was not permitted, save for the few items related to personal hygiene and dress that Betty insisted she have. When she made the mistake of keeping a note she'd received from Mike Lamota in English class tucked between lined pages in a three-ring binder (Your hot, do you want to go Out), Bill found it on

his nightly rounds. He didn't wake her up; she found
the scrap of paper glued to her forehead in the morning
with industrial-strength adhesive. When she tried to pull
it off it rent the skin. She had to go to school wearing the
fragment stuck there, a banner of nonsense over her eyebrows, patchy with blood. She scrawled over the clumsy
ballpoint words with a thick felt-tipped marker on her
way to the bus stop, which saved her from specific
humiliation though not from general.

After this episode, pursuant to threats of a lawsuit
directed at the school board, Bill removed her from
school, on the premise of acquiring a tutor. To this position he appointed himself, and it was no longer difficult
to get away from him, but impossible. If he relented it
was never for long: the span of a measly hour was too
much to ask. All day long, while Mr. Kraft worked, Estée
was locked in with her mother, whose foul nest full of
detritus choked her and gave her swimming headaches.
Though in all else Betty strove toward a pristine ideal,
she could not be bothered to have herself moved from
the bed more than once a week, when the custom-made
sheets were taken by a maid, shaken in the backyard to
expunge accumulated filth, and laundered. The bed had
a toilet beneath it, specially constructed, whose flush
lever was set into the wall within arm's reach. A panel in
the frame of the bed, button operated, slid back when
excretion became necessary. There were no common
bedpans for Betty. Her bed linen was constructed with
fitted holes to make room for the plumbing apparatus.

The nature of her ailment? Medical experts hemmed
and hawed and said it was in her genes, her history, her

makeup. Yet there were some who claimed it was self-inflicted, that Betty Kraft condemned herself to paraplegia. No coincidence was it either that her wedding night had been the start, stated Dr. Joy the family psychiatrist, fired after one session. Once led to bed by Bill, penetrated and fertilized, she stayed there and refused to move. Was it the shock of violation or, as Dr. Joy was overheard to intimate, the laxness of postcoital bliss that laid her out for good?

Estée heard Betty's version of the tale told over and over. 'Your father got me on the bed,' murmured Betty dreamily, twisting in her hands the neck of one of the fat Persian cats she raised from kittenhood and strangled absently. Estée watched as it sputtered, tongue protruding. 'He pulled out the manacles and chained me down, spread-eagled.' For distraction from these inappropriate disclosures Estée would sing, inside her head, 'I can't hear you, I can't hear you,' to the tune of 'Exsultate, Jubilate.' Religion was forbidden in the household but she had seen it on TV. The library was full of it. She liked to sit in a carrel in the audiovisual section, holding the padded headphones to her ears, and listen to the choral voices rise in harmony as her eyes skimmed over the pages she held, where ganglia and Malpighian tubes were pictured in gross magnification. Luckily her father had never been to a library, or he would know temptations lurked there, under the innocuous guise of lepidopterology. He had been surprised when, after her first visit, she told him there were whole rooms of books.

'I'm a self-made man,' he proclaimed, and left it at that.

But the tide of Betty's words could not be stemmed. 'He took it out of his fly,' she wailed, 'and beat me with it till my jowls hung down like a basset hound's.' Estée knew that, like heroines in the old movies Betty favored, she was expected to fall on bruised knees at the bedside, clasping a weak maternal hand to her own tear-stained cheek. Instead she kept her sympathy in reserve, awaiting the advent of reliable sources.

For visits from relatives, including her blind grandfather and a great-aunt with halitosis, Estée had to groom her mother, dress her, and affix to her bald pate, by means of glue, one of the wigs from her collection, which ranged in style from pageboy to beehive. On alternate Thursdays her mother Received. Reclining beneath her canopy, features painted into a ghoulish approximation of vigor, Betty ushered in her guests with a gracious beringed hand while Estée stood shyly behind the bedroom door. Mrs. Kraft had freshened the atmosphere with clouds of aerosol Glade, so that the visitors, on arrival, would cough, choke, and move toward the window to inhale. 'Don't open that!' Betty would screech, for natural light was her curse. The sun was unsubtle and would show her up in all her sad dilapidation.

'How's my baby daughter?' Estée's grandfather would croon, his eyes on Betty while he tossed a gift to Estée. These gifts were always records of old musicals – *Oklahoma! Carousel, Singin' in the Rain* – the scores of which he claimed to have written in his youth. 'But it says here Rodgers & Hammerstein,' Estée objected. The old man cut her off. 'I wrote 'em,' he said shortly. 'Wrote 'em right off the top of my head.' It made no difference, since the gifts, which were no use anyway to someone who had never seen a record player, were confiscated by Bill as soon as his doddering father-in-law was down the front steps. 'Into the furnace with these little fellas,' Bill would say fondly, and Estée never saw them again. She imagined he carted them off to work the next day and threw them in the mix with a dowager deceased of multiple sclerosis.

How long could her parents persist? It was no use trying to talk of reason to them. Her father even knew more Latin than reason, though he believed it to be a lingo invented recently by specialists for the sole purpose of referring to moths. He was impatient when she forwarded the notion that there had once been an empire. 'Don't believe what you read,' he cautioned. 'Lies and lies . . . I could tell you lies. I know guys who bring their kids up on a diet of the stuff. Never forget how lucky you are, Esty my girl. Take a walk through a church, they'll have you believing in justice. Nothing but a sales pitch. Romans, Romans, everyone knows they speak French.'

She practiced secret prayer, a rite not unlike masturbation. Her father warned her it would drive her blind. 'That was what struck down your granddad,' he whispered, out of earshot of Betty's room. 'God, God, and more God. He went against the laws of nature and now he can't see a foot in front of his face. The Protestant old fuck. Excuse me, Esty, Daddy said the *P* word.' The prayer was conducted alone in her bed, in silence, with the utmost concentration. 'Dear Lord, I am under strange government. There are devils here who masquerade as saints. And they are clearly insane.'

Her mother's birthdays were celebrated with extravagance. Pretty Bettys emerged from eight-foot cakes, later
to be fondled by her father in the hall for generous remu-
neration. 'Today your mother turns thirty-nine,' Bill
announced every year. 'Bring on the dancing harlots.'

Betty chose the occasion of her fifth thirty-ninth birthday to initiate Estée into the private club of womanhood.
'Onanism is healthy,' she confided, manipulating invisible parts with an agitated hand beneath her blanket by
way of demonstration, as Estée, humiliated, hummed
'Ave Maria' in her head. 'It's really the best way, and
absolutely safe. When you're older I will show you the
devices.'

She became her mother's procuress, in charge of new
acquisitions for the Betty shrine. She made calls about
auctions, when Betty Grable's toothbrush or hair curlers
went on the market, ordered memorabilia by mail, investigated by modem new venues for the purchase of Betty
Boop cels and Betty Friedan first editions. Betty gave
voice to a series of repeated themes, whining plaintive
solos that sounded polyphonic, like fugues, like sym-
phonies, like bagpipe serenades. 'Have you found the
shower curtain yet? Have you found the special mailbox
decorated with her name? The leaflet the girdle the oven
mitt the Negro ceramic the doggy bone the apron the pot-
pourri sachet the baby book the ashtray the urn the
poster the tampon the grass from the grave?'

At 3:30 on Sundays the bell rang for cocks, and Estée
joined her father in the open air in order to observe the
carnage. The number of cockfights grew as their audience diminished, until no one was present but Mr. Kraft

and his daughter, whose attendance was mandatory. Over loudspeakers Bill blasted out 'The Charge of the Light Brigade,' which he supplemented occasionally with a personal reading of 'The White Man's Burden.' True, he was not a man for poetry, he owned. But in former times Kipling, like him, had been a soldier, he claimed. He could also recite the first lines of 'The Gettysburg Address.'

The rooster death toll mounted until gaming birds had to be shipped in from Arizona. Estée's tolerance for fowl was tested past the breaking point. She had no more condolences for their final thrashing minutes, a veteran of too many gravel-pocked gizzards hanging by a thread, too many curled snakes of intestines, gall bladders, and pancreases in the sand. Even the eggs, incubating under heat lamps, and the newly hatched round-eyed chicks in Easter fuzz struck no maternal chord. She had to look elsewhere for her compatriots – to the bust of Betty, to the moths, to an army of imaginary martyrs. The dead of past centuries, like stars, were peers, perennial and silent. She recorded them in her electronic diary. 'They might not be alive right now, but the possibility of them is alive. It is the same as a memory. History includes every combination. I have already been here ten thousand times. I'm dead, I'm dead, I'm here.'

In the evening, after Bill retired, she carried out her tasks in solitude till bedtime. He banned her from the library when he became suspicious of it; thus she had no access to information save those few necessary bulletins from the outside that pertained to Bettydom and moths. The modem was her only avenue: the Kraft household had entered the information age early, due to its spatial isolation. But she was fined for searching out irrelevant data. 'Ten bucks for twelve minutes Esty?' he thundered, the bill shaking in his hand. 'What were you doing? Were you downloading bullshit Esty? News, current events? I told you, everything you need is here. How do you know this stuff is real? Never trust what you read. It's lies. They got whole books that are nothing but lies, they tried to fob 'em off on me when I was your age, Peter Pan and shit, a bunch of lies on purpose. I'm the only one that tells you what's what. This comes out of your allowance.'

Since she had none it was gentle punishment.

Her first jailbreak effort was disorganized, pure impulse, and resulted in her capture five miles down the road by Bill, who zoomed after her in his goliath Cadillac, into the trunk of which he bundled her with no further ado. The second was better orchestrated but came to a sadder end when Estée, who had taken with her a lode of resalable jewelry, a wallet of crisp fifty-dollar bills straight from Betty's chest of drawers, and a small Vuitton suitcase belonging to same, tried out hitchhiking and was hit upon by a Confederate trucker who told tales of the South before the Civil War. 'When nigras was in their place,' he drawled. She asked him to let her off and in response he bundled her into the back of the cab, dressed her in a stinking, ratty ball gown, called her Scarlett, and licked her feet with Red Man in his mouth, his right hand down his pants. After that she was deposited at a McDonald's and the trucker made a quick collect call to her father, who drove out and picked her up.

With that her quota was made and she resigned herself to marking time.

Her father's guns had names. He took them down and polished them on Saturdays, all the while conversing with their infrared night scopes or matte-finish grips. 'Now you be careful, Simon maboy, or I may just move you over there beside Jigaboo,' he would scold a semi-automatic, tsk-tsking and shaking his head. Estée would tiptoe off while he spoke, along through shining halls and archives where she expected to see, one dawn, the flocks of winged bodies shedding their pins, passing like ghosts through their glass sarcophagi, and flying in pale clouds of color to alight on her father, covering his face and cloaking his arms, binding his legs in a vast cocoon, and bearing him, wrapped in their homespun shroud, aloft to oblivion.

Bill, by accident, let her watch a show on TV one day about people living in an apartment, leading lives that must be standard. The people said stupid things and laughter came from nowhere like a miracle. It was the laughter of crowds, like the men that used to come to bet on the cockfights, who laughed loudly when Bill said something or gave them all drinks. The actors did what they wanted, went to and fro, out their front door and in again. She saw that luck eluded her, though it lunged into the paths of charlatans, flapping its arms and smiling.

Her birthdays passed unnoticed, unlike Betty's, but she was glad to have the luxury of fading from sight. She had been exhausted since before she was born, her embryo, the far-flung molecules that constituted the idea of her, dragging themselves through fields of gravity with untold weariness. She looked for solidarity in the snippets of news she was permitted, items she heard when she borrowed a Sony Walkman radio from a temporary maid, when she bought a magazine from a pizza deliveryman by bartering a pearl barrette of Betty's: routinely, other people too were forced through squalid tunnels of someone else's devising. It was a maze run by perverts and idiots. There could be no protest: only, at long last, emergence into daylight.

Waiting for the new world, she compromised whenever danger crept near. Capitulation was natural, but she feared it. Invasion robbed her of herself. Boundaries were fluid, water and air exchanged atoms, she was unsure where she ended and the others began.

The moths, at first just one more pound of flesh off the lumbering mass of her father, horrible adjuncts to his tyranny, became objects of sympathy as soon as her scholarship saved her from having to eat them. In the face of her erudition, Bill no longer had recourse to scare tactics. She handled the lepidopterans gently, regretted piercing their corpses with her superfine pins. She attributed speech and character to them. 'Excuse me,' a polyphemus would suggest, 'be careful, I'm dead.' Handmaiden moths admonished her with sighs of defeat, decrepit viceroys talked about the kings and queens of exotic countries, a webworm told jokes. There was nothing else to do in her boredom. Silent dialogues with the dry carapaces consisted of connections made too quickly to be said, dismissed before fruition. Bill had another approach: he appropriated all things, exercised droit du seigneur even beyond the boundaries of human flesh.

Inanimate and animate were one: black Rugers could be
called homeboys, a weak .22 was named Flossy, there
were assault rifles named Arnold and rifles christened
Ronnie, dying cocks referred to as Minor and Major,
Jewboy, Polack, and Spic. She watched him and made
sure that her own lonely conversations didn't reek of
ownership. Bill's was a cruel, one-sided alliance against
helpless matter.

The claustrophobia of her routine was mitigated only
by the fact that Bill was more and more distracted, making forays by airplane to collect his own specimens. He
brought them back alive, tens or hundreds beating their
wings against the mesh of compartmentalized lodgings,
mating and fighting through the grilles. He came home
with cocoons, mourning cloak pupae suspended on a
branch by their cremasters, a silken nest constructed by
American tent caterpillars, over which in dark and furry
pandemonium they writhed. He was the hunter, she was
the taxidermist.

Bill spent weekends in Mexico, warm summer weekends when the house was soft in his absence and the
maids moved more lightly in their duties, carrying
through passageways muted laughter and snatches of
Spanish. Fans whirred overhead, stirring curtains and
the scraps of laundry hanging in the atrium on clothes-
lines. On the evening of the solstice Estée watched a
sunset from the second floor, a wash of tropical orange
and mauve falling to the horizon. She overlooked the
landlocked structures of crematorium, refinery, and
power plant, their ugly daylight hulks turned into silhouettes. In the black and the orange she felt like

ascending, trumpets behind her, into the dome of the sky. She thought: Without him we weigh nothing, there's no gravity at all, I can float. Let Betty lie in her bed, nothing can touch me. She projected onto the air in front of her the vision of her own rising body, her wings unfurling from her sides, the sails of boats, but then there was noise, shrieks. She turned and rushed to the stairs, where two maids were hovering at the bottom of the grand spiral staircase, their burdens of dirty towels and silverware abandoned on the floor.

Betty was sitting astride the banister, chest pressed against its length. She pulled herself up bit by bit, bare, psoriatic scalp exposed, mouth smeared with lipstick. Her legs, thought to be atrophied from disuse, clutched together, toes curled, feet meeting through the interstice of rails; she made mewling noises, interspersed with grunts, which signaled she was not displeased by the friction between smooth wood and the angry grip of her pelvic muscles. She clambered in grubby desperation, pulling herself along by sheer armstrength, her knuckles white.

'Let me help you down, you'll be hurt,' said Estée, reaching out to take her hand. Betty growled and brandished a salad fork, the dull tines of which she inserted forcefully into her left knee. The knee was bony, but still a limp tab of flesh gave purchase to the fork, which stuck out almost level with the ground as Betty continued her rutting. It took all three of them to pry her off, kicking, mumbling, and biting with toothless gums, and carry her up to her bed so that the knee could be attended by medicos.

Mr. Kraft, on his return, was furious.

'Would Betty Grable be caught doing that?' he was heard to explode in milady's chamber, after firing the maids for their roles as witnesses. He told Estée he held her responsible. 'But she can walk,' said Estée. 'She can walk, she got there by herself!'

Bill caught her by her shirt collar and shook her until he was tired. When he put her down she had a dislocated shoulder. 'Your mother,' he shot out in parting, 'is a sick sick sick sick woman. She can't do *one thing* for herself.'

Betty was incommunicado for the next week, but when Estée was summoned she came out, in wary stage whispers, with a different account of the events. 'Didn't you know?' she asked Estée. 'That's when I walk. I walk when I'm in estrus.' Estée hummed the Agnus Dei aloud, but Betty failed to notice. 'It's not perpetual with me,' said Betty. 'The call of the wild, I feel it and I make good. For that I can rise from my fetters.'

'Can we talk plainly just for once? Let's can the crazy shit,' said Estée. 'You're either paraplegic or you're not.'

'The stupid deafness of the young,' said Mrs. Kraft, and shook her head with condescending mien. 'My place is in this bed. Why can't you see I have a kingdom here?'

'Do you feel this?' said Estée, and felt around until she hit her mother's knee beneath the quilt and comforter – the pocket of fat the salad fork had pierced, where there was still a scab. 'Do you feel it or don't you?'

'Not a twinge,' said Betty.

'This? This?' and blows were rained down on the thighs, the ankles, the feet.

'Why nothing, absolutely nothing,' protested her

mother, straight faced, appearing, in her casual indifference, to be genuine.

It was an impasse. Lying in bed, Estée wondered if,
when she closed her mother's bedroom door behind her,
there'd been an exhalation, grimace, and slow release of
tears, the invalid rocking back and forth in her
disheveled hills of linen, biting her lips and nursing,
stroking with patient hands, the intricate patterns of
pain.

For Bill the stakes had risen. He hired construction
workers and electricians, the foreman of whom, a potbellied, inky-armed simian, stood guard outside Betty's
door while the others built fortifications. A second door
was built beyond the first, with a built-in alarm to be trig-
gered by anyone emerging from the room who did not
punch the proper code into a digital keypad. Access to
the room was easy, but exit was by number only.
Numerical knowledge alone would get you nowhere,
though: the second door was sixteen inches thick, with a
metal bar across its midriff. Brute strength, therefore,
was also required. Bill put his daughter on a weights
program, installing a Nautilus machine in the basement,
so that her own exit would be possible and the diurnal
visits to Betty could continue. 'I'm not an irrational man,'
he said. 'A mother, a daughter, there's a bond there.
Blood is thicker than your polystyrene.' In the mean-
time, while she was building up her biceps, the foreman
would heave the door open as she went out.

Since the bettors had deserted him, Mr. Kraft went
hunting on his own. Rubbing doe musk on his face, the
urine of red foxes into his armpits, Mr. Kraft stalked elks

and bucks and brought their heads home to hang on walls inside his trophy room. His supervisorial duties at the crematorium were slight: he delegated authority and his rounds were just for show. He watched to make sure that expertise prevailed, that there were no unseemly congresses between the employees and the deceased. On a day of inspiration he would roll up his sleeves and get down to work himself, to show the others how it should be done.

Estée was advised that she would inherit the establishment: to her would go the long rows of incinerators and metal drawers, and before long Bill would train her in their ways. She would start at the bottom and work to the top. Bill would practice what he preached, would take the necessary dose of his own medicine, because he too – and the plan was in his will, in black and white – would be burned to a crisp in the furnaces. He assured clients of this for persuasion, and it did the trick. For a hard sell he would take out a sealed copy of the testament, always freshly updated, and proffer it for their perusal.

When the second door outside Betty's room was completed and fortified, and Estée was bench-pressing eighty, Bill decided to give up the roosters. 'The grand finale,' he told Estée, 'is gonna be a blowout. Company picnic, all the employees. IBM has 'em, other companies too. It's good for morale. Serve 'em up some slop, give 'em a show. Give 'em a run for their money. Strictly speaking those fights are illegal, but I'm my own man. Those guys work for me, biting the hand that feeds if they gabbed about it. Your cockfights are some good clean family fun.'

Barbecue pits were set up, striped circus tents, a sea of folding chairs. To each worker from the crematorium, with his family in tow, was assigned a laminated badge and tickets to redeem for plates of food. The herds were ushered in through a makeshift parking lot on the plot of bare ground adjoining Kraft land, and they entered warily, prodding their children in front of them. A long line straggled out from the solitary Port-a-John. The program consisted of spectacle first, food last. Cow and chicken pieces simmered on the grills and barbecue smoke floated over the cheap seats, exciting salivary glands while the audience waited obediently for the show. Estée sat beside her father in a royal booth, a balcony on the second floor from which a banner hung: *Velut arbor ita ramus*. Moth lingo. 'The branch is sorta like the tree, is what it stands for,' explained Bill.

Tape-recorded bugles sounded. The banner was raised to expose a huge screen. When the cocks were let out they were followed by the lens of a camera and the action was replicated, in extreme close-up, on the enormous screen. A gouged eyeball was presented in Technicolor, its gaping socket four feet high. Confused spectators turned in their seats and muttered to each other. For accompaniment Bill played 'Pomp and Circumstance' from mammoth speakers set into the window frames at the rear of the house.

Bill stood on the balcony, straight-backed and regal. 'Now that's a sport,' he crowed. 'Now that's a damn good fight.' Wagers had not been made, but he professed love for the sport itself, the graceful ballet of evisceration, complete with pirouettes and pliés. When Estée shut her

eyes and turned away from the screen, Bill pinched her
slyly till she opened them again. Squawk, flap, feathers
churned, the combatants were staggering maimed. Their
strutting slowed, they flopped and heaved on the hen-
pecked sand, they were limp and bleeding, one blind.
Estée glanced over at the ringside seats, where frantic
families played at censorship. Mothers covered the faces
of their sons with flat hands, with peekaboo fingers, or
scolded them until they looked away; fathers played
patty-cake with female toddlers in desperate distraction
measures. A few weak-stomached couples escaped to
the parking lot, with surreptitious glances toward the
balcony.

When the roosters collapsed, feathers skittering across
the chairs, into hair and pockets, a stray gizzard pecked
into fragments on the dry earth, Bill saluted and the
screen blipped to black. Spectators were slow to rise.
Hamburgers and pepper steaks piled up on festive plat-
ters, but no guests gravitated toward the grills. Chatter
was kept to a minimum. Bill descended from his platform and mingled with the hoi polloi, making ad hoc
speeches on the lawn, hands clasped across his bursting
abdomen. 'How'd you like it, put some iron back in
your pecker, John? Bob it was? Iron in your pecker, Rob?
Fine animals, yessir. Fine animals. Got guts. We know
that for sure!' Wanly smiling, his employees stood with
restless arms slack at their sides, their children clinging
to their legs, eyes fleeing nervously to right and left.
Behind her father Estée hovered, watching the wave he
made as he advanced through the throng, people pulling
away.

Soon they fled in droves. Their cars jammed the vacant lot and a rude cacophony of horns and raised voices drowned Bill's speechifying. Estée stood motionless, soaking herself in the residue of the crowds, their normalcy, the relief afforded her by the evidence of their disgust. She lived in a nuthouse, it was confirmed, yet she was not insane. Stow away in a Volvo? It would never succeed.

A blue-clad member of the cleaning staff picked up a rooster carcass and carried it to the boneyard next to the generator, where, pinching her nose, she tossed it onto the pile. Estée watched her pick up a nearby shovel and throw a couple of clods of soil onto the corpse. The soil was rich in red worms and their casings, which sped the process of decomposition. Estée knew her worms.

All the grilled meat was still laid out on the long tables. It would putrefy, uneaten by the Krafts or their support personnel. Already the chairs were being folded and stacked, the tent was collapsing in undulations of green and white. The maids laid it out flat on the grass, folded the corners into halves, quarters, eighths, sixteenths, stepping nearer and nearer to each other as they folded. Finally it was a bundle that fit into the arms.

'Why'd they all take off?' demanded Bill of the air. 'Food not good enough for these ingrates? Fire 'em! Fire 'em all! Those management boys won't stop me this time, nosir, litigation my ass. Monday morning they'll be scrounging up scraps from the gutter. Manners Esty. No one has manners anymore.'

She faced the banner *Velut arbor ita ramus* and the gigantic empty screen. There was Betty, at her closed bay window high above. She was crouching on all fours. A flimsy nightgown fluttered on her arms.

Estée envisioned a suicide leap, a shattering plunge through the glass. 'What are you doing?' she called urgently from beneath.

Her mother shook her head, mouthing, 'I can't hear you.'

'Then open the window! How did you get out of bed? And what are you doing?'

Her mother mouthed, 'I can't hear you.'

'Then just open the window!'

Her mother mouthed, 'I can't hear you.'

'Would you please open the window?'

I can't hear you.

two

Bill was overcome by transports of hatred. He underwent a swift reversal — the click-change of scenes through a Viewmaster. There was no slow evolution. He woke Estée up in the small hours smashing displays. Roused by the noise she padded out in T-shirt and bare feet, but her soles encountered splinters and she had to retreat, to watch him from the doorway. 'Ugly bugs! Ugly bugs!' he shouted, tearing moths off the walls, stomping, waving his arms. When he was finished there was not a display case left intact. 'Scorched earth,' he yelled at his daughter, and performed a clumsy dance amidst the ruins.

He left the gallery in chaos, glass and wood and pin-stuck moths all over the floor. To get through the hall Estée had to navigate over the wreckage, careful where she stepped. At 8:00 A.M. maids were already stooping and sweeping.

He posted a note on her bedroom door.

The Specimens are grose, vile repugnant Creatures. The Management will no longer be maintaining a Museum for Them. However we will continue our Study. You will resieve

you're Instrucsions here. You will Create a chart for the
Specimens and record there Progress on this Chart. Specimens
shall be numbered from One on. You will be supplied with
Live Specimens for you're Experiments. You're first
Assinement is to put Specimen One, a mamber of
Acrolophidae, in a jar and Keep Him there by Starvation
until he is Dead. Write down how long it Takes and what
you're observations. Love, Dad.

Estée was initially confused by this directive. Bill
explained to her, while she hefted free weights, that the
work of preservation had changed its course due to his
recent revelation – viz., that moths were hateful, disgusting, and possibly alien. Their provenance might, for
all he knew, be another planet. He suggested Mars off
the top of his head but indicated that he had little interest in further speculation. The workroom would be
converted into a laboratory. He would keep a steady
stream of live moths coming in. Her job, as his assistant,
was to corral them in a variety of habitats and subject
them to experiments.

Every evening a new specimen, every evening a note
with instructions. On a clipboard she would keep a journal. 'In the records,' said Bill with great effort, 'you tell
what they act like when you do stuff to them, for me
plus also for science in general. For the future history.'

'I don't *want* to experiment on them,' she ventured
boldly, fully expecting a physical assault. Bill stood over
her as she completed a cycle of knee bends, his midriff
her sky above.

'Honey,' he gravely intoned, 'it is for the good of the many. The experiments we do are for Posterior.'

'We're not biologists,' she said. 'We don't know the first thing about experiments. No one experiments on moths anyway. We know about them already.'

'How did Mary Curry invent tuberculosis? How did Alex Bell invent the phone? By accident! Discoveries happen when you least expect it.'

He would not be swayed from his mission. She tried to ignore him, but he threatened to withhold food, to prevent her access to Betty, and finally to lock her in her room. She decided to comply.

Bill's notes told her to sequester moths in jars, without food or air; to drown them, burn them, dissect them. He had shelves constructed, with dividers between the numbered sections. Each moth remained in its section even after it had died. She had to spray them with insecticides, feed them poisoned food, remove portions of their bodies while leaving others intact. She had to closet them with predators: spiders, beetles, frogs, lizards, birds, even rodents purchased by her father from mail-order suppliers. On one occasion she had to insert the head of a cat, presented to her in a shoebox, into the mesh cage of a tiger moth and catalog their joint deterioration. The lepidopterans were provided routinely with dung, chitterlings, and pickled pigs' feet. Bill wanted to reform their eating habits: he had never trusted vegetarians. They preferred a lingering death.

'You're not going to change them,' she argued. 'It's evolution. Their digestive systems weren't made for meat.'

'Esty,' chided Bill, 'your lepidopterans can adapt. Survival of the fittest, Esty.'

She made careful entries on the chart. Her father bade her read them aloud and would nod sagely and say, 'Ah, oh yes,' as she read.

Number 32 has sacrificed sections of both maxillary palpi in his efforts to escape the jar. He has abandoned all fungal matter and appears to be ingesting nothing. All his energies are directed toward freedom. Number 41 is bereft of both wings on the left side. Her right eye is severely damaged from constant pressure against the side of the can, yet she stubbornly persists.

Bill ordered books for her with which she was able to bone up on the biology of butterflies – life cycles, food, and natural habitats. In some cases, she could delay their deaths by making small adjustments, unbeknownst to the boss. But usually there was no balm for their suffering, and she watched them shed their parts until they were nothing.

Mr. Kraft bought her a high-priced microscope, a digitized scale, an antique Bunsen burner, and a handsomely laminated poster of the periodic table. She had no use for them, but Bill was pleased by the expansion of his high-tech lab. He was prepared to make additional expenditures to keep it, as he said, State of the Art. Estée could invoice him for whatever tools she wanted. 'Science is advancing,' he said as he tweezed the wings off a monarch.

Mrs. Kraft, behind her double door, wished to hear

nothing of the proceedings. She had her shrine, and telephone calls from old friends. Frequently, when Estée
came into her room, she was telling a story to a child-
hood pal in Baltimore or a relative in Orlando. 'There we
were, in the kitchen with apple pie à la mode,' she would
say. 'The golden retriever was lying at the hearth, and
Bill leaned over to me and said, "God bless America,
sweetie pie, I sure love you."' Her decay had acceler-
ated; she had no appetite, forgot to wear her teeth, and
repeated herself four or five times whenever she spoke.
She ordered Estée to keep sending off for Betty artifacts,
always said, 'Yes, yes,' with a nod and a sweeping hand
gesture, 'Buy it, buy it, buy buy buy,' but when the items
came in she paid no attention, letting them accumulate
on the wall, on top of tables, littering her room.

Estée adopted a policy of non-interference. She was an
adjunct to the whims of Bill and Betty, whose schemes
were as random as laughter, as senseless as an accident.
She disavowed all connection to the tasks she performed.
'Dear Diary: the Age of Majority. I saw it on TV. I will
leave here and be in the world. I will see the normal
people in malls and on the street. Normal people will be
everywhere, teeming.'

For the lab experiments, she found that Betty's training
came in handy. She went though the motions faithfully,
all the while remaining, in secret, cold and motionless,
inanimate. She identified with walls, chairs, tables, any
collection of atoms turned callously to function.

Bill made a concession to her new maturity by allowing her three hours of television viewing per week,
which she used to watch the news on CNN since she

was not allowed access to print media. He decried all so-
called facts set in type. Almost everything presented to
you on paper, he said, was a falsification, the product of
numerous conspiracies between corporate and government interests vying for positive coverage. There had
never been, for example, men on the moon. 'Plain as the
nose on your face. Trick photography,' he asserted, wolf-
ing down spareribs with sauce dribbling over his porous
chin. 'News is just like any other show. All done for
ratings, girl. For bucks.' As a businessman himself he
was in on the game. He was wise to their schemes. 'Sure,'
he said modestly, 'if I was in that line, I'd be a straight
guy. I'd probably get crucified. You know what a stickler
your dad is for the truth. But I'm not, I'm in cremation.
And there too I'm just as honest as the day is long.'

The bombing of Hiroshima and Nagasaki was another
popular myth. 'There's no such thing as a nuclear bomb,'
stated Bill over a megabowl of ripple chips. 'That's a line
they cooked up so they didn't have to have as many
wars. It's a doozy. You got a lotta folks fooled on that one,
but me and a few other guys know the deal.'

Bill was no longer a purposeful strider, the man who
in younger years had warded off naysayers and skeptics
with the square set of his shoulders. Now and then Estée
caught him in confusion: hiding under a pile of coats in
the foyer, speaking in a referee's booming tones, he
would arbitrate a tussle between himself and himself.
The coats would roll and quake. He gave himself split
lips and bruises and chipped one of his bottom teeth
with a fist. When she caught him at it he would shrug his
shoulders and continue his struggle, strangling himself

until his eyes bulged while she looked on. He groped and blundered in broad daylight; surprised during acts of lunacy by a maid or deliveryperson, he kept up his activities until they wandered away again and then subsided into a stupor. She found him grappling with Betty's bedroom door one night, delivering a soliloquy. 'She took it from me. Give it back!' He noticed Estée staring from the shadows and whistled nonchalantly. 'It's my heart kid. Weaker than it used to be, can't get the damn thing open.'

'I'll open it for you,' she offered, but Bill took his hands off the door and stepped back shaking. 'No. No way. A man does these things by himself.' Later he denied all charges.

Still, he had the presence of mind to leave live moths for her nightly. With hundreds of specimens dying or dead in their cages in the lab, he liked to visit while she worked and stick a finger through the mesh. Some of the early captives still refused to shuffle off, remaining in their small demesnes without eating or flying, huddled against the wall with wings folded, resolutely though barely alive. Bill was fascinated by these fighters. 'How's that rascal 76?' he asked at breakfast almost every day, for Number 76 had held on for months in a state of fossilized morbidity. He was covered in dust, he had lost all his legs and half his thorax, but still when Estée blew gently on him his antennae quivered, out of keeping with the wind.

Thursdays Estée had the evening off and Bill would catalog the night's new specimen for her, setting it up in its habitat and initiating the round of punishments. On Good Friday in the spring before her eighteenth birthday,

she came into the laboratory and found that Specimen
Number 228, trussed up with ropes, legs bound, in a
cage against the wall, was a dog.

> **Number 228 will be disected live as per Usual procedure
> starting with Feet. It is a Miniture Snauzer. It will Not be
> Sedated if thats what your thinking. Tools for this Esperiment
> will be found in supplys Cuboard. Please begin Immediately.
> As I will Brook no Delay. Thanks alot, love Dad.**

The muzzled schnauzer craned its neck and looked at
her through plaintive eyes. She unbound it, removed the
muzzle, and let it out of the cage. It trotted happily at her
heels as she left the lab.

She found him in her mother's room, where he sat
beside the bed reading slowly to Betty from a picture
book as Betty's right hand, always busy under the sheets,
fomented dissent in an unseen quadrant, causing her to
breathe rapidly and lick her lips. 'Little Pig, Little Pig, let
me come in,' read Bill, ignoring the commotion. 'Not by
the hair of my chinny chin chin.'

'Won't do it,' said Estée right off. 'No way.'

'Now honey,' he said. 'Let's not bother your mother.
We'll take this shoptalk outside,' and he closed the book.

Betty only had eyes for the schnauzer. 'Pooky poo!' she
said, and patted the quilt beside her. The dog leapt up,
wagging its tail.

'He wants me to cut off its feet,' said Estée. 'Can I have
some support from you for once?'

'Oh dear,' said her mother, and stroked the dog's head
with her free hand.

'Taking it outside,' said Bill in his warning voice, rising.
'Come on.'

'We can discuss it right here,' said Estée.

'Let's not make trouble,' said Bill.

'After all,' said Betty, 'there's a lot of little doggies like
this one.'

'Forget it,' said Estée.

'The penalty for mutiny is walking the plank,' said
Bill. 'In the King's Navy, it's hanging by the neck.'

'We're not pirates,' said Estée. 'There's no king either.
We're American citizens in the twentieth century. We
don't torture dogs. I can call the ASPCA in fifteen seconds flat. That's where they take care of animals. I found
it in the phone book.'

'Dear oh *dear*,' said Betty. 'Father knows best.' She
picked a frilly baby bonnet out of her bedside drawer
and affixed it on the dog's head, tying the pink ribbon
under his chin.

'It's for the sake of progress,' said Bill. 'How about
those guys with monkeys and electrodes? Defense
Department, those guys do 'speriments on half a million
critters every year. No one calls the ASPCA on them.'

'You don't have a license,' said Estée.

'License, schmicense,' said Bill gruffly. 'What's the
difference? Up the evolutionary scale a bit. There's
plenty of stupid critters around. Dumb beasts Esty. Cool
down.'

'I'm not going to let you,' said Estée. 'I draw the line at
higher mammals.'

Bill grabbed up the dog, which whined in his arms, its
bonnet falling lopsided over one ear.

'For this you're picking a fight with your father? This little overgrown rat? Its brain is the size of a walnut. Come to your senses!'

'Absolutely not,' said Estée. 'If you want to talk senses, I'm ready.'

'I'll break its leg right here and now,' said Bill, and started to twist its paw. The schnauzer screamed and bit him. He let it drop. Estée retreated beside it as it limped into a corner.

'You try that again and I'll knee you in the balls,' she told him, gritting her teeth.

'Oh my,' whispered Betty.

Nursing his wounded arm, Bill shook his head. 'Sharper than a serpent's tooth,' he said.

She was able to pick up the whimpering dog while Betty, playing Florence Nightingale, kissed Bill's bite wound and emitted coos of sympathy. She left the room, ran to the front door, and let it out. 'Go away,' she yelled when it lingered on the steps. 'Just go away!'

Bill was subdued for a few days, and then left a raccoon in the lab. This was followed by an opossum. Both of them she carried outside, in their cages, and loosed on the lawn. She and Bill began a speechless battle. Nothing was said about the new specimens, nor about the notes that accompanied them.

This Specimen #231 is a Very Mean Giunea Pig, note the Large Incisors. In Various countries this pig is Eaten after Stewing, plus it is Kept as Pets. Please flay 25 Strokes per night until Death occurs.

Number 232 is a Lop Eared Rabbit. This Specimen will be Garroted with a Coat Hanger but not killed, then make it run in a Whole bunch of Circles.

Afraid that grisly fates would befall Specimens 231 and 232 if she released them in the backyard, Estée transported their cages into her bedroom, where she fed them scraps of lettuce from the kitchen. Bill didn't ask where she'd put them. He'd abandoned his practice of coming into her room while she slept; she'd bribed a carpenter to install a lock and wore the key on a shoelace around her neck. Anyway, his concerns had shifted; he was preoccupied. Obviously it no longer occurred to him that she was any-where when she was out of his sight. When she retreated she dissipated like vapor; a fading feature of the land-scape, she diminished unnoticed as the scene changed. Bill's paternal neglect resulted less in melancholy than relief.

Though they hardly spoke as the weeks passed, Bill checked the moth charts. She kept up her observations of the lepidoptera as their few remaining representa-tives, one by one, gave up the ghost. No new moths appeared, and the stubborn importation of mammals decreased until it happened only once a week. She had a collection of rodents in her room, six in all, and had freed a weasel, a stoat, three cats, and a poodle when her father disappeared.

'Where is he?' she queried Betty, who'd had herself transported on a stretcher to her sunken bathtub and, imagining herself Ophelia, languished there with flowers scattered on the water and the tresses of a long wig floating on the bubbly surface around her head.

'Your father is everywhere,' mumbled Betty, brushing at the wig with an affected air, her eyes, adorned with fake lashes, shuttered closed.

'When's he coming back?'

'Your father never leaves, Estée,' said Betty. 'He's with us all the time. Would you hand me my mirror?'

She stayed in the bath until her skin was waterlogged and began to peel off, at which point she allowed the maids to lift her out.

Number 76, the last of the faithful, was the only moth left alive when Bill returned from his hunting odyssey. He had a special treat, he told Estée, taking her aside when he came in the door. 'The specimen to end all specimens. It's the big one, kid,' he bragged, and rushed for the kitchen to pop open a beer and swig. His face was gritty, mottled with sweat and dirt. 'Breaches of security will not be allowed. You will not be leaving the house till the specimen's been experimented.' He ushered in a corps of four burly security guards and ordered them to post themselves as sentinels at the front gate, the front door, outside the first-floor windows.

'I will bring the specimen in through the back door and afterwards one of these fine gentlemen will be on guard there too,' he said to her in confidence. 'Luckily we have the weekend to ourselves.'

'I don't condone this,' said Estée. 'I'm not your ally.'

He dismissed her protests with a wave, chucked his half-full beer can through a window, and went out. She watched him reverse a rented van up to the back door and trundle in, on a dolly, an eight-foot box covered in

white cloth. The portals were closed after him by a uni-
formed man, wooden faced, bearing truncheon and
holstered revolver.

Estée retired to her room, where she locked herself in
and read an old history textbook. 'Copernican theory dis-
placed the ancient Ptolemaic system, in which the earth
was at the center of the universe, unmoving.' One of her
mother's Valiums improved her mood till boredom
moved her, eventually, out the locked door again and
into the kitchen. She was snacking on Doritos and boot-
legged Coors when Bill snuck in behind her, put her in a
headlock, and dragged her to the lab. A crowbar lay on
the linoleum beside the open crate; inside, on a bed of
straw and foam, an old woman was curled, snoring.

'Specimen 243, *Homo sapiens*,' said Bill proudly.

'You're a fucking lunatic, said Estée.

'Language!' reprimanded Bill, casting an eye upon the
woman, and clapped his hands in glee.

'You can keep me here,' she told him. 'But you can't
make me do anything.'

'You can take notes,' suggested Bill.

'I'm going,' she said, and turned to leave the room.
Bill performed a flying tackle and they landed in a
painful sprawl. Her back hurt, her chin bled. She'd bitten
a ridge in her tongue when she hit the ground and Bill's
weight, pinning her beneath him, more than compen-
sated for his poor muscle tone. 'Jesus Christ, get off!' she
said, and elbowed backward till her funnybone crunched
his nose.

Bill bellowed and mooed, a wounded steer. He rolled
off her and staunched the flow of blood with a dust rag

he dragged from the counter. Leaning into the crate, Estée shook the old woman's shoulders. 'Wake up!'

'Ha ha hee' giggled Bill, with a nasal twang. 'That won't do anything. Shot a trank right into her main line. A tran-kwee-ly-zer.' He wore a small goatee of blood.

'Who is she—?'

'Old bag. I found her selling Bibles in Tulsa, and crappy pictures of angels. Religious comic strips.'

'You're letting her go,' Estée said, but again she'd mis-remembered Bill's strength. It had been a mistake to try straightforward defiance; a devious path would have been wiser. Her father was a fat man, some might say obese, but that didn't stop him from charging. He had the strength and mass of a bull, the speed of a human cannonball. He was on top of her again in seconds, press-ing thick thumbs against her windpipe.

She woke up with a headache and swollen tongue, her back sore, across the room from the old woman. They were both caged. She sat up, put her hands on the bars, and threw up. Bill pulled life-size cages from his hat. He was a prestidigitator. Had he planned the operation in advance, reckoning on her resistance? Was the old woman merely a ploy? Red-herring bait for the real prize? Specimen 244: daughter.

'I'm not surprised,' she said aloud.

The granny raised her head. She was thin and grimy, potbellied and bleary. Her white-crusted eyes were gummed shut.

'I'm sorry,' ventured Estée.

The woman blundered around in her cage, feeling at the bars. 'Hello?' she quavered. 'Hello?'

'Hello,' said Estée. 'Can you hear me?'

'Are we at the hotel?' asked the biddy. 'In Bermuda?'

Senile; possibly blind.

'Excuse me. Can you see?' asked Estée.

'See? See what? Where's my beads?'

'See anything?'

'See everything. I seen it all,' said the woman. 'Is this the presidential suite?'

'Presidential suite, oh yeah,' said Estée. 'What's your name?'

'Margaret! Margaret. Tell me the view.'

'I can see white sands,' tried Estée. 'Tall palm trees, date palms, and the water's green. There's a cool breeze when I lean out.'

'I've always wanted to come but they said I couldn't go,' sighed Margaret, pulling at a matted gray lock. 'They said I couldn't because of the money. The people at the hostel, those mean girls. That bitch Maria, and she was dead wrong. Tribulations! Trials! I knew I'd get here, the Lord made me a promise. Did we fly?'

'We sailed on a cruise ship,' said Estée. 'It's beautiful here.'

Margaret sniffed and nodded, her iron smile unflinching.

'A couple's lying on the sand. They're tanned dark brown, wearing swimsuits. Their skin's shiny with coconut oil, can you smell it?'

'It smells good enough to eat,' said Margaret.

The door opened and Bill stood over them, a tray in his hands.

'Room service,' said Estée.

He handed her a sandwich through the bars.

'I don't want it, can't you see I was sick? And how am I going to go to the bathroom?'

'A chamber pot will be supplied,' said Bill.

'Don't they have modern plumbing?' queried Margaret.

'It's the simple life,' said Estée. To Bill she whispered, 'What are you doing? Let me out. I won't go anywhere.'

'If you're not part of the solution, my girl, then you're part of the problem,' he said, waggling a finger in warning.

'But what are you planning? Come on.'

'Ho! That would be telling,' said Bill. He shoved an apple through Margaret's bars. She dropped onto all fours and felt around on the floor till she found it.

'I would like a Wiener schnitzel,' said Margaret with her mouth full. 'And a Rhine wine. Dry. And I'll take the whole bottle, waiter. Tell him to bring the whole bottle.'

Bill picked up a pointer from the countertop and poked her thighs and stomach through the bars. She dropped the apple and cowered at the back of her cage. 'Stop poking! Make him stop the poking,' she shrieked. 'This hotel has bad waiters.'

'Physical fitness,' said Estée firmly. 'It's to improve your cardiovascular endurance.'

'Stop it anyway,' grumbled Margaret, her arms up protecting her face.

When he left them alone Margaret polished off her apple, drank the water Bill had left, announced she was having a siesta, and went to sleep again. With a neck cramp and one foot full of pins and needles, Estée counted the pocks in the hardboard ceiling tiles and computed the average number of pocks per tile. She tried to discern signs of movement from the cage of Specimen 76 against the wall, and finding none memorized portions of the periodic table. 75. Re. Rhenium. Atomic weight 186.2. 76. Os. Osmium. Atomic weight 190.2. She played at establishing a correlation between Specimen 76 and osmium. The atomic number of osmium was 76. There were 76 protons in the nucleus of an osmium atom. Specimen 76 was the longest-lived of all the specimens she and Bill had subjected to pain. Did it signify? Seventy-six was also the name of a chain of gas stations. Gas – osmium – octane? Ga-O-O. Ga was the abbreviation for gallium, and O for oxygen. Possibly she had hit on a formula. GaO_2. A miracle molecule? A secret yielded up by chance?

Exercises were futile. Tedium blurred the surfaces, the counter and the fluorescent bulbs in their white metal casings. She dissected the sandwich, lined by Bill with rancid salami and yellowed mayonnaise, and threw it through the bars.

Margaret stirred in her sleep and muttered, 'Hot, hot, the spaniel.' Estée was longing for change, any change. She fell asleep watching fleecy white grannies leap over picket fences, counting them as they baaed.

Bill woke her up by rattling her cage. It was night and he was a ghostly Michelin man, nude and white.

'How long are you keeping me here?' she asked him groggily. 'And her? She's blind. Plus she's senile. How long?' In her sleep, Margaret moaned. Bill munched on a moonpie.

'Until I prove my point,' he said, licking a crumb off his lip.

'And what's your point?'

'I have it here,' said Bill, and lifted an envelope, 'but it is highly secretive. Though at the same time, if I may say so, it is widely understood by geniuses. Such as yours truly.' He stuck it through the bars. 'You may read it after I leave. I will flick the lights on.'

'Just tell me what you're doing. What?'

'A test, whaddya think?' said Bill indignantly, and snuck off, his buttocks flopping like dimpled saddlebags on the flanks of a pack mule.

4 Truths

1) This Old Bag is Genus Homo Sapiens. Homo Sapiens in general are all Secret Aliens. Proof: SAPIENS-ALIENS If you change a P for a L the Word Alien is Hidden in Sapiens!!!!

2) An Alien does Not feel Pain.

3) Aliens are Enemys.

4) "We have seen the Enemy and He is Us."

5) Solve this clue: Ima dog

'Please call room service for my potty,' said Margaret. 'I gotta go.'

'Room service can't come yet,' said Estée. 'They're having a problem in the kitchen. You have to wait.'

'Can't wait,' said Margaret. She squatted and urinated in her cage.

'I'm sorry about this,' offered Estée. 'It wasn't my idea.'

'Some enchanted evening,' warbled Margaret softly, 'you may find your true love.'

Bill came in with breakfast trays after Margaret had sung three verses.

'Shut your trap, granny,' he said.

'Let me out,' said Estée. 'This is ridiculous. I'm not going to run off.'

'Got my guards out there, you couldn't go if you wanted to,' said Bill, and unlocked her cage. She crawled out and stood up, then stretched and ran to Margaret's cage, but Bill was ahead of her.

'Let her out too,' said Estée.

'Hold your horses,' grumbled Bill, but he opened Margaret's door and, while Estée hoisted her out, laid down paper towels to soak up the pool of her urine. Margaret roamed around the room, bumping into things, and then sat down cross-legged on the floor to eat her grapefruit. Estée leaned against the counter, drank the coffee Bill had brought, and watched him drag a spool of twine from the supplies cupboard. He hammered three-inch nails into the linoleum, four of them in a large rectangle. Margaret ignored this, smiling and nodding. 'You hear the wedding bells?' she asked Estée.

'Bells, yes,' said Estée. 'A white church with a steeple, on the beach.'

'You may see him dancing . . . across a crowded room.'

'What are you blabbing about, you stinky hag?' asked Bill. He dealt her knee a quick kick as he knelt down to tie twine to a nail. 'Your religious crappola? I'll show you who's boss, not some old faggot with white hair and a dress.'

'What a lovely vacation,' said Margaret, and spat out a grapefruit seed.

Bill attached four stout lengths of twine, with a lot of slack, to the four nails. He made them secure with many complicated knots and then fed their ends through four small plastic collars. He took the grapefruit rind away from Margaret and snapped one of the collars around her right wrist.

'Jewels?' she said, and went compliantly to her bondage. 'Lovely. They are fit for a queen.'

He snapped on the second collar, and then the last two to her ankles, around the grimy bobby socks.

'She reeks,' he remarked.

'Some enchanted evening,' sang Margaret, and smiled.

Bill pulled out a plastic groundsheet and cut a hole in it. He put it over Margaret's body, with the hole over her face. 'For observation of the subject,' he told Estée.

'You may find your true love.'

'She's revved and ready to go,' said Bill approvingly. 'Don't try anything. I'm going out, but I'm locking the door behind me. Back in five.'

'What's the young man doing now?' asked Margaret, as he went out.

'A mud pack. For the skin.'

'Some enchanted evening . . .'

'Don't worry.'

'. . . you may see a stranger . . .'

She was spread-eagled, arms and legs splayed. Estée knelt beside her and patted her arm.

'You may see a stranger . . .'

Bill came back in pushing a dolly loaded high with bricks.

'The mud packs,' said Estée nervously.

'Here we go, here we go,' trilled Bill.

'Come on,' Estée urged him. 'You don't need to hurt her. Your theory is true, completely true. Who needs to prove a truth? I believe it 100 percent.'

'It's not enough to believe,' said Bill. 'You have to *know*. I know I'm the boss. She doesn't think so now, she'll know it soon. Seeing is believing.'

'She knows. She knows, she's just senile.'

'You think she knows? Then what's that bullshit? You hear that?'

'Across a crowded room . . .'

'Write this down,' said Bill. 'Experiment on Subject 243 began at 9:32 A.M.'

He started piling bricks on Margaret's abdomen.

'Are you taking me dancing?' she asked Bill, blinking.

'He's submerging you in the mud and then you soak for a while,' said Estée. She smoothed the ratty hair on Margaret's temple.

'Shut up,' said Bill. 'No bullshit. Stand back. No inter-ference! Mediation could wreck the whole thing.'

'Some enchanted evening, when you find your true love . . .'

As the bricks weighed her down Margaret sang louder. They stacked up in a pyramid on her midsection.

'. . . when you hear her laughing . . .'

'Shut up,' said Bill, heaving three bricks onto her pelvis.

'Stop!' said Estée, grabbing them off again. Bill cuffed her hard and she fell back, hand up to a bloody nose.

'. . . across a crowded room . . .'

He dropped a brick on Margaret's mouth and then

picked it off to survey the damage. Her lip was split and teeth might have been broken, but she licked the blood off. Estée watched her eyes glint from between the near-closed lids, darting back and forth as the chapped lips puckered and stretched.

'. . . then you will know, you will know even then . . .'

'She's a beaut, ain't she? Now who's the boss, you old sow? Who's the boss?'

'. . . the sound of her laughter . . .'

Bill was dropping the bricks now. They fell on Margaret's legs and chest, gouged her forehead and slid off.

'. . . will haunt you again . . .'

Estée scuttled backward on the linoleum and struggled to her feet, retreating toward the door. Bill had forgotten to lock it when he came in with the bricks. She opened it and was out in the hallway, home free, dashing for the telephone in the foyer. She dialed 911 and ran out the front door. She paced on the porch, wiping blood from her nose. No one came. Maybe they were driving slowly. The Kraft house was set far back from the street, but beyond the palm tree border she could see the orange cast of a streetlamp. Otherwise, dark and silent.

'Police!' she yelled, but no one answered. Finally, shivering, she went back inside. The guards had disappeared.

In the lab, nothing was visible but bricks. Bill must have trundled in a second dolly: at its peak the pile was as high as her waist. Bill stood back, his arms crossed over his protuberant belly. 'Experiment concluded at 10:28 A.M.,' he told Estée. 'Write it down. The subject showed a complete lack of awareness of masonry weighing her down. The subject was dumb and insensate.'

'But where is she?' asked Estée, and started to pull off the bricks. Bill drummed his fingers on his stomach and then rooted in one ear with a pinky. She dug through bricks until her fingers were raw.

'We showed 'em who's boss Esty. Me myself and I.'

'But she has to be there,' said Estée, digging with frantic hands. She could find nothing but bare floor.

'Number 76,' announced Bill gravely, 'is deceased.' He raised his hand to Estée and showed her the last of the moths, dangling single-winged between thumb and fore-finger.

'What happened to Margaret? Where did you put her?'

Bill shrugged and flung Number 76 carelessly to the floor as he exited. Estée dropped to all fours and kept scrabbling through the bricks, but nothing lay beneath them. Rotting salami was scattered and trodden under-foot.

Despairing, she repaired to Betty's room, where she found her mother knitting a cat-sized sweater. The bed was hung with crepe-paper streamers, and Betty sported a frilly pink pinafore. 'A little party for your father,' she chirped. 'The man is a martyr to science,' and as Bill descended on them, for once decent in a dressing gown, she cast away the needles and opened her arms. 'Here we are!' she said brightly, hugging Bill to one side of her and Estée to the other. 'Just one big happy family.'

three

Bill threw Betty out with the bathwater. He referred to it later as spring cleaning, though it took place at the beginning of summer, the year Estée labeled T-1 in her diary to signify approaching freedom. One afternoon she entered Betty's boudoir to find it empty. The shrine had been dismantled, the bed stripped, the closets laid bare. An alcove formerly reserved for wigs housed a vase of fake flowers.

She confronted Bill in the dining room, where he was chowing down on a super-duper macaroni meal, his old standby.

'Where is she?'

'Your mother has gone on to a better place,' said Bill haughtily, orange powder on his chin. He ate the cheese powder straight from the package, without bothering to melt it.

'Where? What better place?'

'Details, details,' grumbled Bill, but coughed up the name of a clinic in Fort Lauderdale.

'It's very nice here,' said Betty when Estée reached her by phone. 'I get pedicures, and a specialist comes in to give me hair-replacement treatments. I highly recommend it. They have shuffleboard, but I don't play.'

Estée broached the subject of postsecondary educa-
tion, but Bill would not hear of it. He prevented her from
applying by refusing to sign the forms stating she'd had
a tutor. She dropped the idea and planned only on
escape: eighteen in December.

'We are seceding from the Union,' Bill announced a
week later.

'Excuse me?' she asked.

'What I said,' said Bill. 'I am starting my own country.'

'Don't you have to have a revolution?' asked Estée.
'You can't secede just like that. We're in California, not
Texas.'

'I will use whatever means necessary,' said Bill. 'It
will make the tax situation difficult, but I will talk to the
lawyers.' He appointed her his second-in-command.

'I do not wish to participate,' said Estée stiffly, to no
avail.

The new regime, Bill decided, needed first a flag;
next, a declaration; then citizens, laws, and a military
force. Estée had a change of heart about involvement:
she would play along, hoping he'd be remanded into
police custody as soon as he crossed the line. She envisioned him sending armed patrols into the neighborhood,
there to rob and pillage, and planned to bring in the
authorities as soon as this occurred. She looked forward
to the instant of triumph. With Bill incarcerated and
Betty institutionalized, she could strike out for foreign
parts.

Bill was not artistically inclined, so the flag was a
stumbling block. He hit upon the notion of using the
Velut arbor ita ramus banner, but dismissed it owing to

the alien connotations of the moth language. 'Aliens will not be allowed into the country,' he told Estée, 'except as emissaries or slaves.' Eventually he decided to rely on the family name and had the word *Kraft*, cut off a mac & cheese box, silk-screened in bold hues onto a giant sheet of cloth. This he flew from the roof on a mast built onto the TV antenna. He forgot to tell the silk-screeners to customize the logo, so the flag read 'Kraft' in blue block letters surrounded by a red border, and beneath this, to the right, ®.

He put up a customs booth at the front gate, employed three security guards who wore Kraft crests on their breast pockets, and instructed them to halt all incoming traffic and demand passports. On the first day of this regime the maids were turned away; the next day Bill corrected the oversight by issuing special entry visas. These were Bill's handiwork and consisted of a piece of paper stating, 'Enter One Alien into the United State of Kraft, sined, Commander in Cheif Bill Kraft.' Bill's orthography had not improved with his new status.

The maids did not read English and were under the impression, Estée learned from a guard, that the measures were purely for household security. Bill was delighted to have guards. He found himself well suited to be commander in chief. Drawing on stock capital, he expanded his forces, hiring eight additional security guards to live in full-time. They were his private army, well paid. They wore tailor-made Kraft uniforms, complete with Kaiser Wilhelm helmets. The helmets were heavy metal and hard to breathe in; the troops griped until Bill gave them salary hikes.

Estée watched Bill hold debriefing sessions in his war room and observed the men's unconcerned silence. At the back, they exchanged the sports section under their seats; one did a crossword puzzle while another flicked dirt from beneath his fingernails. Corporal Martinez, Bill's favorite, confided in Estée after a rigorous drill under Bill's command, 'I save up – *¿como se dice?* – for one dry-cleaning business with my brother, I clear out when I got enough. Is a secret, okay?'

Bill had given up science and embraced the political life. He eradicated every trace of the laboratory and the moths and concentrated on preparedness. He outfitted his army with weapons from his blooming homegrown armory and supervised target practice. The constitution took a backseat to might: 'Before you know what to do, you gotta be able to do it,' he strategized to Estée.

She herself was busy with affairs of state, since Bill had nominated her for the post of United State of Kraft attorney general. She played the role of private secretary to the chief. Bill dictated letters to state senators and members of the House of Representatives in which he outlined his plan to secede. He stated that he was a property owner and entrepreneur: he owned his property outright, and should thus be allowed the privilege of self-government. 'I bought up the place,' he dictated to her for the form letter, 'it's mine. No one owns it but me. Why does a guy pay taxes? So other guys can shuffle papers in Washington? I don't need the service, so why should I pay for it? If war comes we in Kraft will defend ourselves to the hilt with no help from the U.S. of A. Let's face it. You don't need us, we don't need you. This camper isn't going to keep paying out one-third of his income just for garbage collection.' He announced his intention to discontinue the custom of paying out monies yearly to the Internal Revenue Service.

Sure, he conceded: while the matter of his secession was pending he would continue to disburse funds to the income tax pool. Once it was approved, however, he would expect a full refund from the treasury, including accumulated interest at the prime lending rate. In his letters, he included no return address, signing *Bill Kraft* with a magnanimous flourish.

'They're not going to say yes,' Estée warned him.

'I'll take it into my own hands,' stated Bill. Estée kept her smugness to herself, awaiting the rebellion that would settle his hash. She was careful with the letters she typed up and inserted, here and there, an occasional veiled threat of bloody uprising. Bill did not read over the communiqués sent in his name, so she had license to exaggerate freely, making frequent reference to Bill's private army and reservoir of munitions. She became a clock-watcher, waiting for the bomb blast.

Commander Kraft, who decorated himself with five stars, was cautious when it came to stockpiling defenses. He moved his armory from a coat closet into a room in the basement that was hidden behind a concealed door. His guards were issued their guns and ammunition at 7:00 A.M., and after the armaments inspection at night the guns were impounded. Each round of bullets used in practice was counted. Guards who did not perform well at target practice were assigned special tasks and forced to shoot more often. Bill had standards.

He discovered Estée's collection of salvaged rodents
three weeks after he'd built his customs booth. She left
her bedroom door unlocked when she went to the bathroom and when she got back Bill was squatting by the
row of cages.

'What are these aliens doing here?' he asked.

'They're from before,' she told him. 'I keep them in
reserve. In case their country needs them.'

'Hmm,' said Bill. 'Unauthorized.' But he was not displeased. A country should raise its own livestock.
'Self-sufficiency Esty. You don't wanna pay for imports.
Need a trade surplus there on your agriculture.' Since the
hamsters, guinea pigs, and rabbits were not fit for breed-
ing or herding, he would appoint them foot soldiers in
the ranks of his reserves. 'Uniforms, Esty. That's what
these men need.' He exited and returned with lengths of
string and Kraft crests. 'Hang these around the boys'
necks. Identification, Esty. Dog tags we call 'em,'

'They won't stay on.'

'Inspection every morning at eight,' said Bill. 'When
you get up.'

Estée took hold of a struggling guinea pig and tied a
string around its neck. It defecated.

'Hey Esty, see that? Its shit looks like its food.'

Next Bill decreed that she would be his information
minister. Without information, how could they make
laws? Kraft was a nation with only two human citizens,
plus a third who was currently on foreign sick leave,
and a standing army. Estée's job was to gather facts for
the purpose of establishing written statutes, as insurance
against a future in which the citizenry might expand

and grow disobedient. 'You can see the news for two
hours per day,' he stipulated, 'and I will relay its message
to the troops.' The Kraft triumvirate, including its hon-
orary first lady in absentia, would serve as the liaison
between the common men of the armed forces and the
world outside.

'We will watch it together,' said Bill, thumbs through
his belt loops, rocking back on his heels, 'and I'll say the
important parts to you, and you can be my speechwriter.
Every night after weapons detail I will address the
rabble. I will give them the news of the day.'

Excited by the chance to expand her horizons, Estée
agreed to the proposal.

'The United States consumed eighty thousand peta-
joules of energy this year,' related a toupeed newscaster.

'Write that down!' said Bill, clapping a hand on her
thigh. Estée wrote it down.

'This is equal to the total consumption of Africa, South
America, and Europe combined,' continued the newscaster, and turned to greet his co-anchor cheerfully.

Bill dictated his report on the item while counting
bullets and reshelving .357s.

The U.S. has consumed the energy of Africa, South
America, and Europe he stated.

'What are you talking about?' asked Estée.

'You can't say mumbo jumbo to the common people,'
said Bill. 'Got to make it easy on 'em. You heard the man
Esty. That's the news.'

The next day Bill delivered a speech on the impor-
tance of sound foreign policy. 'We gotta do like they did
in the Persian Gulf War,' he said. 'You go out there, you

take what you need. We call it assistance. I'll keep you posted on future developments, boys.'

The troops listened slack-jawed and bored to these addresses, delivered by Bill from a podium in the war room. They snickered at the back, refused to participate in the Q & A sessions at the end of the lectures, and shuffled off to their quarters as soon as the last word was out of his mouth. Since they were an army of eight, their barracks fit nicely into spare bedrooms.

'Commander,' said Estée after their second demonstration of indifference, 'don't you think we could just install a TV in the mess hall? Then they could watch the news while they were eating.'

'Esty, Esty,' said Bill, 'that would mean disaster. They're not ready for that. We have to protect them.'

During a speech on Muslim holy wars, Bill admonished his troops kindly to steer clear of Arabs. 'You got your Hussanes, your Godoffies, your I-told-ya Coemanies,' said Bill. 'They're the worst kind of aliens, next to your Papists, your Protestants, and your dirty Wops,' said Bill.

Murmurs of discontent arose from the fray and Corporal Martinez got up and left the room.

The next day Estée inserted into a letter from Bill to the secretary of defense the sentences 'I am going to kill them all. I have many guns in my house, including assault rifles.' It was the hour for bold measures. She licked a Love USA stamp and stuck it firmly on the envelope, writing Bill's return address in the upper left-hand comer in clear capital letters.

'The deployment of peacekeeping troops has been

characterized as a strategic follow-up to the 1990 deploy-ment in Saudi Arabia, which was the largest since Vietnam,' said a commentator. Bill sat forward on the couch beside her, eager as a Boy Scout. 'Air force assets include F-15 fighters, F-16s, F-111s, and F-4s; also F-117A stealth fighters, B-52 strategic bombers, and A-10 tank busters.'

Bill donned his blue cap with gold braid, commanded Estée to summon the battalion, and addressed them in his war room. 'The United State of Kraft will be sending you to Kuwait, where you will join American aliens in a project to siphon all oil out of holes in the ground and bring it back here,' he announced proudly. He was removing kitchen funnels from a plastic bag when there was a rustle of disturbance in the ranks.

'I'm quitting,' said Corporal Martinez, looking around at the others as he rose from his seat. 'I had enough of this shit. You're fucking crazy, man. I'm outta here. They should put you away.'

His brothers-in-arms, shaking their heads and mutter-ing, also rose from their chairs. Kaiser Wilhelm helmets dropped and rolled on the carpet.

'Is this an insurrection?' sputtered Bill, clutching a funnel in his chubby fist.

'We're quitting,' said Corporal Randall. 'We want our paychecks for this week before we go.'

'A mutiny! You're traitors,' said Bill, blinking rapidly, at a loss.

'You're bullshit,' said Corporal Randall.

'You will return your weapons! And your uniforms!' squeaked Bill.

'We don't want your fucking lame-ass uniforms, buddy,' said a corporal with sprouting facial moles, and spat on the carpet as he quit the room.

Estée stood by with arms crossed while slumping Bill, a study in defeat, watched the men file out.

'Napoleon wouldn't stand for this, Esty,' he said. 'You're my attorney general. They can't do this. You stop 'em!'

'There are always people to hire,' said Estée. 'They have the right to quit.'

'Oh no, oh no,' said Bill. 'They're defecting! You can't quit the army.'

Estée followed him as he scuttled out the door, clutching the plastic bag in his hand. He went upstairs to the barracks, where the men were throwing clothes into overnight bags, and ordered them to surrender their weapons. He waited, chafing his wrists nervously, till these were in a pile on the floor and then hefted one of the guns and waved it in the air.

'C-c-court martial!' he stuttered, high pitched as a choirboy.

'Fuck off, man,' said Corporal Randall, who had exchanged his uniform for jeans and a Budweiser T-shirt. He headed for the staircase, his compadres taking up the rear.

'Halt!' quavered Bill, and fired one shot into the ceiling.

Corporal Randall jumped at the noise and turned around.

'You can't do that, asshole. What are you gonna do, hold us hostage? We'll call the cops on you. Serge, go call the cops.'

Corporal Serge edged toward the dining room.

'Stop!' said Bill, and fired into the doorway. Serge stopped. 'They have no jurisdiction here! This is Kraft!'

'Fuck off,' said Corporal Randall. 'This is the U.S. of A., loony tunes.'

'You shoot again, loco,' said Corporal Martinez, 'and you could have some serious trouble.'

'Commander,' said Estée, 'why don't you just let them go? What we need is brave, loyal men, which these are obviously not. We need soldiers worthy of the State of Kraft. We need to handpick them, not just call up some security company out of the yellow pages. It's time to ring out the old, ring in the new, am I right Commander?'

What can you expect from aliens,' conceded Bill, though his hand still shook on the gun's molded grip.

'I suggest we carry out an exhaustive search for non-aliens to serve in our military,' said Estée. 'Get these guys out of here. What good are they doing? They were always layabouts. They were always slackers. Am I correct, Commander?'

'You may have a point,' said Bill. After a pause he hiked up his belt around the tent of his slacks and motioned the corporals toward the door with his gun. Estée watched from the front door as he followed them down the front walk, out along the driveway to the customs booth in the yard. Gun in hand, Bill watched them disperse down the street to their cars.

He was quiet for several days. 'Diary, he's left high and dry. He can't mount the revolution now, which means I'm stuck with him. I folded under stress, afraid of

casualties. I missed the chance to foil him. Another plan
is needed to send him over the edge.' Bill's mantle had
been stripped off rudely, leaving him trembling. Restless,
Estée gave him a pep talk.

'Remember, those were Americans,' she cajoled over a
Pop-Tart breakfast. Bill was consuming the whole box.
'Of course they want to undermine you. They might even
have been spies. They were jealous of your kingdom.
You have to rise above it, Commander.'

Bill poked pensively at a slab of microwaved bacon.

'My reserves,' he said. 'The furry pigs and those rabbits.
Are they also Americans?'

'Strictly speaking, no,' said Estée. 'They are citizens of
the world.'

'The problem with the reserves,' said Bill, 'is they can't
bear arms. They can't take orders Esty.'

'That's true,' allowed Estée. 'But not for lack of trying.
I mean those reserves have their hearts in the right place,
it's just they don't speak English and they don't have
opposable thumbs. They would if they could, I know
that much.'

'As an interim army,' suggested Bill, 'they might be
all right. Don't you think?'

'They would be fine,' said Estée. 'Until you can find
non-aliens, which might be a big job.'

'Big? Colossal. I don't know one person besides myself
who's not an alien. You can't trust anyone. Your mother's
not cut out for governing. She's not a leader Esty.'

'You can trust me,' she said. 'Can't you?'

'Okay,' said Bill, pushing his plate away, pieces of
Pop-Tart floating in bacon fat. 'Please assemble the

reserves, in full uniform, in the briefing room at ten hundred hours. That will be all.'

The guinea pigs and rabbits proved recalcitrant. They would not respond to leashes, so she carried them two by two to the war room, where she set them on chairs with food bowls in front of them. While waiting for Bill they gnawed at the green pellets and peed on the vinyl. Estée cleaned up with paper towels and kept the soldiers in their places. They wore their Kraft crests around their necks on string, but these were easily dislodged. She had to reattach the crests every few minutes, after surges in rodent activity.

Bill marched in at the stroke of 10:00 A.M. and saluted the troops. 'I understand that, as citizens of the world, you do not speak or understand American. All your orders will therefore be given in a visual form,' he announced from the podium.

He broke into a hopping, jiggling dance, resting only to draw sketches with chalk on the blackboard behind him. A rabbit hopped down from its chair, a hamster scuttled beneath a radiator, and Estée kept busy reclaiming them, maintaining a constant vigil for emerging pellets and moisture. Bill liked his soldiers to be neat. She moved between the seats, cleaning up pellets and wiping, retrieving AWOL pets from the floor as Bill performed a loosely choreographed charade in the background. It was exhausting labor.

Finally Bill pronounced his platoon formally debriefed, saluted, and walked out. She closed the door behind him, sat down, and relaxed. On the blackboard was a series of arrows, indicating tactical maneuvers, accompanied by rudimentary depictions of rats. On their backs were blobs resembling pineapples, minus their spiky tops. She looked closer and discerned it: the pineapples stood for hand grenades.

She closed the door to the war room behind her and went to find Bill. He was on the front porch, sipping a Heineken.

'I feel we should address strategic flaws,' she said, sitting down on the steps beside him.

'Go ahead, go ahead,' said Bill affably.

'With the, uh, deployment of the grenades there may be problems.'

'We have to give them names,' said Bill. 'I was thinking, Corporal Rabbit One, Corporal Rabbit Two. Like that.'

'They can't pull the pins on the grenades or throw them, is the first problem I see,' said Estée.

'Of course, I thought of that,' said Bill. 'They will be our kamikazes.'

'Kami—'

'If a conflict situation arises,' said Bill patiently, 'the reserves will be hurled aloft. Either you or I will pull the pins in the grenades before this hurling takes place. You and I will both have to practice our hurling.'

'But, but the kamikazes,' said Estée, 'my understanding is they agreed to die for the emperor or something. But the guinea pigs—'

'l have confidence in them,' said Bill, taking a swig. 'I think you were right Esty, their hearts are in the right place. Those brave boys will not shirk their duty. They would die for Kraft.'

'But—'

'I trust the conflict situation will not arise,' said Bill. 'If my petition for secession is granted, it should be no problem. Hostilities will not be necessary.'

'The grenades may also be too heavy for them to carry,' said Estée. 'They may not be able to march if burdened with the grenades.'

'We will not use the grenades in practice drills. I have found an adequate substitute in your mother's old things,' said Bill, and from beneath his chair pulled a plastic L'eggs egg, labeled Control-top Pantyhose, Medium, Beige, Sandal Toe.

'I see,' said Estée.

At weapons detail the reserves were fitted out with their dummy grenades. Bill insisted on taping the L'eggs to their backs with Scotch tape, which circled under their bellies like saddle girths.

'But it'll hurt them when we take off the tape,' said Estée.

'Brave men to the last,' said Bill staunchly.

At first the reserves were confused by their new L'eggs, and then they became nonchalant. Estée noted, however, a marked lack of activity. When the guinea pig sector failed to remain in formation, Bill got frustrated and unleashed his Ruger on a rusty barrel. Estée placed the platoon carefully in single file.

'It's the language barrier,' she amended. 'They have their own methods. You have to give them a little leeway. They're not Americans. That has both advantages and disadvantages. Patience is a virtue.'

'Bullshit,' said Bill, but appeared to resign himself to the disorganization of the troops. Sweltering under the

sun the next morning, and frequently refreshed by Estée
with bowls of cold water, the reserves were trained in
endurance on a makeshift obstacle course. Shepherded
over low platforms, they were forced to negotiate their
way over doll-sized ladders Bill had reclaimed from
Estée's old Barbie play set and then encouraged to wade
through water in a Tupperware container. Estée toweled
them off, adjusted their L'eggs, and gave them bowls of
cold water. She comforted herself with the knowledge
that human guinea pigs were more dangerous: this was
the lesser of two evils.

Bill brought up the subject of disciplinary action, to be
directed against reserves who failed to obey orders. Estée
suggested the carrot would be more effective than the
stick. 'A good soldier knows that punishment builds
character,' said Bill. No, argued Estée, positive re-
inforcement was the way to go with rodents. They were
not strong and were likely to weaken if physically
injured. 'All right,' said Bill reluctantly, 'but if I get one
whiff of insubordination, the kid gloves are off.'

Bill was using a carrot as a reward during a training
drill, for rodents who successfully completed their run
along a treadmill, when the doorbell rang and Estée ran
to get it. She opened the door to two men in gray suits.

'We're with the Federal Bureau of Investigation,' said
the closest one, and drew an identity card from his breast
pocket. 'I'm Agent Wilson, this is Agent Fruehauf. Would
Mr. William Kraft be available?'

Breakthrough. She saw light at the end of her tunnel.

'He's here,' she said. 'At the moment he's drilling
reserve troops in the yard out back. Please follow me.'

The FBI men met Bill, who shook their hands eagerly and claimed he was a big fan of J. Edgar Hoover. Estée occupied herself collecting rodents off the ground and installing them in cages.

'We do have a search warrant for the premises,' said Agent Wilson.

'Be my guest, be my guest,' said Bill heartily. 'Give you the grand tour.'

They went inside, Bill in the lead, Estée trailing. The FBI men were stone-faced and bored, following Bill through the downstairs rooms, upstairs, finally into the basement. Estée kept a tight reign on her excitement. Agents Wilson and Fruehauf stooped occasionally to open a cupboard or glance beneath a table.

'We'll need some time on our own, if you don't mind,' said one of them to Bill, who had not shown them the armory.

'Sure, make yourselves at home,' said Bill, all jocular welcome. 'I guess you wouldn't be able to tell me if my petition has been granted? Would you care for a drink?'

The agents opted for coffee. While it was brewing, Estée scrawled a note on a grocery-store receipt: 'Arsenal downstairs concealed door east end pedal operated floor level.' She bunched up the note in her hand and gave it, pressed against the handle of a coffee mug, to Agent Fruehauf, who was staring vacantly out the window while Bill told them the story of his life.

'. . . own father was a crook, a common crook, beat me to a pulp every day of his life, so I took my savings off a pizza job and invested in landfill . . . ,' he said fondly. 'Esty, get your dad a Heineken, would you?'

Estée retired to fetch the beer. Her father was a chameleon of delusions. Not once since the arrival of the FBI had he called her his attorney general.

When she got back with the beer he was beaming with satisfaction and the guests had left their coffee mugs steaming on the table.

'The Americans are responding,' he said. 'They are going to grant my petition, I can feel it in my bones.'

Estée sat with him, nervous, glancing at her watch until the FBI men clumped back up the stairs from the basement.

'Mr. Kraft,' said one, 'if we could speak to you for a moment?'

'In private,' added the other.

'Sure, in the study,' said Bill, eager beaver. Estée waited until they were inside and then stood outside the door, which was cracked open. She could hear well.

'I'm afraid what there's been here is a prank,' said Agent Wilson.

'Misunderstanding,' added Fruehauf. 'An unfortunate expenditure of Bureau funds and our personal time.'

'We're not going to point any fingers, but in future,' continued Wilson, 'since we can't afford to waste our time on jokes, and we don't want to press charges of malicious mischief, especially since we feel there may be a minor involved, but we'd appreciate it if you were careful what goes out of your house. In terms of mail.'

'Oh, dear,' said Bill.

'We received misinformation, in fact several threats, intimations of felonious activities that would come under Bureau jurisdiction . . . of course there's no evidence, it's been a wild goose chase,' said Fruehauf. 'Nothing whatsoever to warrant our involvement. As I'm sure you know.'

'Oh yes, yes,' said Bill.

'This petition you're talking about, we don't know about that, it may be administrative material,' went on Wilson. 'As far as the armaments, the felonies are concerned, you've got a clean slate, so that's where our involvement has to end. We'd just like your help in ensuring that this kind of mix-up doesn't occur again. Discipline, maybe. The help of a counselor. The teenage years can be difficult. Emotional turmoil. We have your cooperation on this?'

'My, yes,' said Bill, bedazzled.

'Thanks for your hospitality,' said Fruehauf. 'We should be moving on.'

Estée, shocked, leaned back against the wall, drawing deep breaths. Agents Wilson and Fruehauf came out the door with Bill at their heels like a puppy and shot her stern looks as they passed. Bill saw them to the door. In a panic she ran through her options, and when Bill returned she was past him in a lash, waving a piece of paper, offering up a staccato excuse. She caught up to the agents on the curb.

'Excuse me!' she said. 'Wait!'

They turned, raising four federal eyebrows.

'Didn't you see it?' she asked. 'In the basement? All the guns? There are grenade launchers, I've seen fully automatics, I know for a fact there are Marlin Model Nines and .45s, SIG P220s and P226s, Steyr AUGs, M-16s, AKs. Doesn't he have to have a license? Isn't it illegal?'

'Honey, said Fruehauf, 'you're agitated. There aren't any weapons in your daddy's basement. He's a little eccentric, but he's a good American. Has he told you about his service in the armed forces? His war service? Did you know your daddy was a hero?'

'War service?'

'Vietnam, sweetheart. Your father was a Green Beret. He was a good soldier. He did a lot for this country in his own way. Head trauma, too bad, but he was a fine soldier once.'

'But I can show you! Didn't you find the door?'

'Sweetheart, go talk this over with your daddy. If you're having problems, you should talk to him,' advised Wilson in paternal tones.

'Didn't you see the floor pedal? Didn't you go in?'

Wilson and Fruehauf exchanged sideways glances.

'No, hon, there's no secret door down there,' said Fruehauf softly. 'Now run on back to your dad. You two need to have a little talk. And you remember. He was a fine soldier once. He paid his dues for the red white and blue. You should be proud of your daddy.

'We have to be on our way,' said the other, and they turned and got into their car.

She stood watching them, despondent, as they gunned the motor and drove off. Was she deluded? Was she as unbalanced as Bill?

Back in the basement, she located the foot pedal, stepped on it, and the door popped open. There was the armory, fully stocked. Her father was perched on a footstool polishing an M92 automatic with tender care.

'Those men didn't come in here,' she said. 'Did they?'

'Oh, sure,' said Bill casually. 'I showed 'em the works when you were making coffee. We're on the same side, yessirree Bob. Two men brave and true.'

'Were you in the army?' she asked him.

'The army is for wimps,' said Bill.

He was a liar, but still he was a mystery she couldn't fathom. Alone in her bedroom, she took out a pocket calendar and counted the days left to her birthday: eighty-one. 'Diary, they are banded together in strange compacts. The police, Bill, and the FBI. They shut me out. Even logic is no defense against them.'

The next morning Bill announced his intention to disband the reserves. They had had enough training, he said. 'Anyway, let's face it, we were just going through the motions, if they're gonna be hurled they don't need to be combat ready. Now do they?'

Estée had lost her zest for humoring him. Evidently it was no master key to liberty.

'Do whatever you want,' she said. 'I'm tired.'

Bill began to wait for the mail with avidity. Its delivery was the focal point of his day. He kept expecting a treaty of secession to arrive. He was convinced the Americans would let him go without a fight. He called the post office when no mail arrived to make sure the carrier had not been struck dead on his route. When, after a couple of weeks of waiting for the mail every day, he'd still received no communication from legislative or executive potentates, he started calling around to try to trace the progress of his request. He called Congress, gubernatorial offices, committees, the White House, the Pentagon, Fort Knox. He called the chamber of commerce in Washington, the

Junior League, the Young Republicans at Georgetown University, the Central Intelligence Agency, the Secret Service, the Justice Department, even Fish and Wildlife. None of these establishments could offer any reassurance.

'Red tape,' he grumbled.

Since there was no end in sight, and she was getting sick of the monotonous passage of time, Estée typed up a brief note and mailed it from the local post office.

'I knew it! I knew it!' rejoiced Bill, galloping into the dining room with his letter as she sat eating a lunch of soup and crackers. 'Read this!'

Estée knew what it said but cast an eye over it and nodded. She had gone for the gold and signed herself, The President. Bill did not trouble himself with postmarks. The note read simply, 'Your request is granted.'

Congratulations,' she told him.

'Hallelujah!' he cried.

four

After independence day, Bill stabilized. He went back to the crematorium, from which he'd been absent for months, and proclaimed an end to Betty's rest cure. She returned from Fort Lauderdale in style, in a rented limousine. Bill had her old room ready for her. She took off her wig and showed Estée the beginnings of the new crop of hair, which rose in clumps from the moisturized scalp, many tendrils sprouting out of each follicle like hairs on the rubber head of a doll. They had cured her at the clinic, she said, of her chronic penchant for self-help. It was understandable, they had told her, that Bill had been displeased by the habit. For a man, they said — a husband — did not like to see being Done Right what he could Do Worse himself. 'They taught me,' Betty confessed, 'that self-stimulation should be done in private, if at all. I hardly ever do it now. I watch TV instead.'

The Krafts would not forget their daughter's birthday this year. Betty announced a gala celebration would be held: her relatives would be invited, and business acquaintances of Bill's.

'I don't want one,' protested Estée, but Betty knew that no meant yes.

Estée was busy planning for her future. With money pilfered from Betty's purse she mail-ordered a strong-box, which she kept beneath her bed. She wore its key around her neck, with the key to her room. Into this box she loaded, when she had the chance, valuables she knew would not be missed, jewelry no longer worn by Betty, bills she found among her parents' belongings. She tallied it up every week, though she could not accurately appraise the value of the merchandise. By mid-October she had a cash tally in excess of $1,200, though the other items were worth much more. She had labored under unfair conditions for years, for the meager recompense of room and board, in manacles and shackles. This was her retirement fund.

Betty sent out invitations and was constantly on the phone to caterers and entertainers. Being an aficionado of country music, Bill had expressed a desire to hire Conway Twitty for the evening. When he learned that this would be impossible, he enlisted Betty's aid in find-ing a country act whose performers would agree to sport Kraft bandannas and avoid all mention of God in their lyrics. That's the one problem with country music,' said Bill, 'they're a bunch of Protestant hillbillies, Jesus Loves Me till the cows come home. But you can't tell artists what to do. They got their heads up their assholes.'

Preparing for her departure, Estée took the five remain-ing reserves to a house down the street and left them on the doorstep in a cage. One hamster had died in a seizure. She counted her funds whenever she was alone and scoured the house daily for portable valuables. Betty's gems could support her for a couple of years;

Bill's old watches would translate into food and rent. It was all in the waiting.

'What would you like for hors d'oeuvres?' Betty asked. Estée said artichokes, *saumon fumé*, and caviar, but Betty told the caterers they wanted lobster on black rye, oysters, and crabs' legs. Betty solicited her daughter's input regarding the decor: 'Would you like streamers in red, white, and blue? Or rainbow colors? Balloons with favors inside?' But when Estée said she'd rather not have streamers or balloons, Betty put in a special order for Christmas-colored crepe-paper curlicues and a tank of helium. The only tack to take was embezzlement, so Estée asked for a party dress and a series of makeovers and squirreled the money away in her box.

The day approached slowly and Estée's diary ran like an inventory. 'October 13: earrings, seed pearl. Eighty dollars? October 21: cuff links, gold and onyx. One hundred dollars?' She prowled through closets, silverware drawers, the pockets of Bill's suit jackets, the desk drawers in Betty's bedroom as her mother snored. To make her escape route smooth, she memorized the number of a taxi company, the location of the Greyhound station, made a reservation at a Quality Inn, studied maps of the freeways into Los Angeles County, and sewed a money belt from scraps of fabric discarded by Betty.

Bill was handling the seating plan for the fete. It was to be a sit-down dinner for fifty, followed by drinks and dancing.

'You got your three basic groups,' said Bill. 'You got your geriatrics, on your mother's side, you got the friends, and you got your money men. Your mother and

me, plus you and the mystery guest, will be at the head
of the table, facing the stage. Geriatrics to our right,
money men to our left. My broker, your mother's brokers,
assistants, lawyers, investors, a sales rep or two, you
know the deal.'

'Friends?' said Estée. 'I told you, I don't have any
friends. How am I supposed to have friends? I haven't
walked five hundred feet without you watching in two
years.'

'Tut-tut,' said Bill. 'Let's not be down in the mouth.'

'I'm not inviting any friends,' insisted Estée, but Bill
was unconcerned.

'How'd you like to sing a song?' he queried.

Her grandfather and the fetid great-aunt arrived on
the eve of the occasion, after driving across three states
from Texas. 'There's my girl,' said her grandfather
when she greeted him. 'Why look, your little rosebuds
have bloomed.' Great-uncles and cousins-once-removed
would be joining them in the morning. Bill put them up
in the barracks, lately fallen into disrepair, but not before
dealing the grandfather a cuff to the ribs.

'You old geezer,' he said when Granddad doubled
over.

'Don't do that, you pig!' shrieked the great-aunt. 'He
has a bad liver!'

Bill added a jovial insult or two and told Estée to show
them to their rooms.

'How Betty could ever have married that bloodsucking
lowlife,' sighed the aunt, depositing her baggage on the
floor. 'Oh, I'm sorry, dear,' she added as an afterthought.
'I'm sure he's a wonderful father.'

Estée watched the minute hand pass 12:00 at midnight and lay in bed elated, assured of her jailbreak,
counting no sheep but feeling, with hands walking softly
over cotton ribbing, nubby seams and mattress tacks,
these well-known dimensions for the last time. She saw
herself borne aloft on the downy back of a gigantic white
bird, its wings moving up, down, up, through the ether,
but she couldn't sleep until she had added a series of
complex knots, bolts, and handles that anchored her
securely to the bird's back. Only after the last lock had
slid into place was she safe in her position, could she
drift off sweetly, a rolling patchwork of green and yellow
farmland far below.

When she went downstairs in the morning, decorators were scurrying around from table to wall to shelf and
standing lamp, frantic and full of their tasks. Ceilings
and furniture were festooned with crepe paper, green,
red, white, and gold: it was a jungle of hideous indul-
gence, banners graven with 'Estée-18' and 'Happy!
Happy!' draped from curtain rods, staple guns wreaking
havoc on the plaster, flowers on every surface. Betty
could not have done worse. In the kitchen, caterers bustled and swore, setting out tiers of glasses and sculpting
huge monuments in succulent fruit. They were putting
trays in the oven, rolling dough and cutting bread, mix-
ing pastes and chopping nuts, grinding fresh basil with
mortar and pestle, blending cilantro and allspice. The
smells gave her a rush, hastened her on her way out the
back door, past the sand lot where the cocks had fought,
past the dilapidated shed where Persians had been bred,
into the boneyard once a compost heap. This to remind

herself that all the normal rush and frenzy of the house, its forced goodwill, was paid illusion.

In the dirt the skulls and talons of long-deceased roosters were still visible. With a stick through the eyehole she lifted a skull. Clusters of tail feathers had not yet decayed and the plumes stuck out of the mound here and there. Yellowed claws curled in on themselves. Gnats circled above the heap in the bar of shade cast by a jacaranda. She extracted a pack of Bill's cigarettes from her shirt pocket, smoked one surveying her old country, congratulated herself, and then threw the butt onto the mound.

'What are you wearing? Let me see you model it!' said Betty, as her manicurist applied gleaming silver nails to her finger stumps. Estée found a dress in a closet in the attic, debutante style and ancient, put it on with difficulty, and went back to be inspected.

'A little more risqué might be nice,' said Betty, 'to show off your attributes, but I guess it'll have to do. And for that you paid nine hundred dollars?'

'And fifty,' said Estée brashly.

She was watching Bill set up a slide projector in the banquet room when one of the decorators, running messages for Betty, came to tell her the rest of the relatives had arrived. Parked behind the catering truck, they were a vanload of elderly people Estée did not recognize. Betty was rolled out to greet them and sat in her chair at the top of the stairs. She smiled, the gracious hostess waiting for them to mount the steps, as Estée assisted a drooling old woman in a dark-blue felt hat. As their progress up the steps dragged on, Betty's bright smile turned into a strained grimace. An old man had reached the summit, his cane tap-tapping at the rail, and tripped on Betty's outstretched foot. Estée helped to steady him and he snaked a hand around her and pinched her buttock. Betty stretched out her arms to him.

'Unca Dicky!' she cooed in a baby voice, and made kisses in the air in his direction. 'Mwuh-mwuh! You're looking great! You haven't changed a bit!'

'The help is getting prettier every day,' he said, gravelly voiced and lecherous, as he pinched Estée's other buttock out of Betty's sightline.

'*No*, that's your great-niece, Estée!' said Betty, offering up a giggle.

'All the better!' said the doddering lech as Estée moved away from his fingers.

'Isn't there anyone my age?' she whispered to Betty, leaning down. 'Don't they have kids? Grandchildren?'

'All dead,' said Betty gaily. 'Unca Dicky had a low sperm count even in his prime. One kid came out mangled. Everyone? This is the birthday girl.' Estée stood beside her, crowded in by the jungle, vines of hanging crepe paper and foliage of balloon clusters, as Betty wheeled around the circle of sedentary relatives and introduced them one by one. 'Your Great-Uncle Randy, Unca Dicky, Aunt Ruthie, Aunt Linette, Cousin Lee-Lewis, Uncle Martin, Aunt Sara, and everyone, this is my daughter Estée, isn't she gorgeous?'

'Oh please,' muttered Estée, but gray and white heads were already waggling from the recesses of overstuffed love seats and high-backed chairs.

'Just like you, Betty,' said a woman with a hairy wart.

'Like a picture,' put in Aunt Sara, and Unca Dicky
made an obscene motion with his right hand under a
bundle of red streamers. 'Nice setup you got here!' Dicky
crowed. 'All with the dough from the sewage? The shit
and the pisspots?'

'You mean *landfill*. Oh, Bill diversified,' began Betty,
and Estée headed for the banquet room. She was interrupted by the doorbell and opened the portal onto an
endless vista of young women wearing lipstick and
dresses, smiling and holding purses up in front of them.

'I'm sorry,' said Estée. 'Who are you?'

'We're here for the party,' said a redhead in the vanguard. 'Are you the birthday girl?'

'But who are *you*?' repeated Estée.

'We're your friends!' said a couple of them in unison,
and a merry titter ran through their colored ranks.

'Excuse me, what?' said Estée. 'I don't have any friends.'

'Count your blessings honey,' said a blonde with large
hair. 'Your daddy hired us,' and they swamped her, surging through in waves of chatter and sprinkles of glitter,
headed for the tables.

Then came the flanks of businessmen, some of the
faces she remembered from the cockfights. They
swarmed toward the hired friends, who were standing in
small bunches near the stage, preening and talking, flopping their hair and stretching casual arms out in
self-conscious poses. Estée helped seat the old people
in front of their place cards until Bill came up and took
her arm.

'This is Peter Magnus. He's in real estate. My baby
daughter, Esty.'

'Estée,' said Estée. 'He says it wrong.'

'Pete,' said Pete Magnus, and shook her hand. He was puffy-faced, shining, and tanned a plastic shade of brown, with a jerky smile. 'Pleased to meetcha.'

'He will be sitting beside you,' said Bill, and then stage-whispered in a rush of gin-soaked breath, 'Mystery guest.'

'Your dad,' said Pete Magnus, 'is one of my clients. New account. He's a good guy though. Your dad's a good guy.'

'Whatever you say,' said Estée, and went to settle a skirmish between Aunt Linette and a red-haired hired friend who was jabbing her in the chest.

'Would you tell this old bag the card has my name on it?' said the redhead between gritted teeth. 'See? Car-la. C, A, R, L, A. Is her name Carla?'

Betty's face, at the foot of the table, was hidden from the rest of the assembly by a huge sprig of baby's breath. Estée sat down between Pete Magnus and Bill, who were discussing a leaseback deal.

'Are those call girls?' she asked Bill, but he was clanging a fork against his wine glass.

'On this special occasion, Esty's eighteenth birthday,' he boomed over the chatter of disinterested guests, 'we're gonna show a slide show later on, after the food. Home movie-type stuff. Memories! Big announcement to make. Now enjoy the vittles. Band's taking requests.'

'What big announcement?' asked Estée.

'Your birthday present,' said Bill. 'Surprise.'

During the soup Estée watched Carla spoon-feed the executive beside her. Pete Magnus leaned in front of her to talk to Bill. 'Ever thinking of putting this place on the market, send it my way,' he offered, while Bill scarfed raw oysters and washed them down with gulps of rosé. Caterers and maids served over shoulders, Betty tried to talk through the baby's breath to Unca Dicky, and the country band played 'Jambalaya' and 'Your Cheatin' Heart.' Carla and the executive made an indiscreet exit leaving napkins crumpled on their plates. Down the length of the table, around the linen corners, played social pantomimes, the call girls making free with spirits and finger food, emitting squeals as suited legs transgressed beneath the table and suited arms jostled bare ones above it, spilling wine and food down their shirtfronts. Pete Magnus, talking debentures, futures, and municipal bonds over sherbet, was cut off as Bill swayed to his feet, the band finished 'Weary Blues From Waitin',' and the lights went down.

'Here we go, Hallmark moments,' boomed Bill, and clicked a button on his remote control. Above the stage a picture flicked from a white square of light. It was a baby in a wading pool, its blond mother holding its hand as the cherub stared openmouthed, round-eyed at the camera, a blowup turtle air tube on its waist, bleached by sunlight.

Bill clicked again and the pool gave way to a picnic scene, another blond mother holding a child in frilly playsuit on her lap, smugly smiling, pinky up its nostril. This brought out a laugh or two, but giggles and gasps from untold points in the darkness signaled guests at other leisure.

The slides followed the child through kindergarten,

skiing scenes, campfires, a family Christmas, a pony ride, then a prepubescent wearing a Hawaiian lei on the deck of a cruise ship.

'But they're not me,' hissed Estée at her father. That's not us!'

'Six of one, half-dozen of the other,' said Bill.

He clicked again and the next slide came up: a pretty girl in cheerleader outfit, blue-and-gold pom-poms and short skirt to match, flashing orthodontic teeth in ado-lescent glamour. Behind her stood parents, their heads out of proportion to their bodies. The heads were Bill's and Betty's, stuck to the smaller-scale figures in the scene.

'This shot was taken at a funny angle,' said Bill. No one cared. Betty was breathing through an asthma mask and across the table from Estée an old man had removed his soiled diapers and placed them on his dirty plate. New couples crept off, leaving the banquet hall behind them. Chairs scraped back two by two.

'The Adirondacks,' narrated Bill. Estée looked up to a vista of pines, a checker-shirted family in the foreground, with blond teenager, face hidden by a baseball cap, and fishing poles. Their faces were Bill's and Betty's, this time matched with bodies even tinier. Bill had never looked so slender. The heads loomed large, hovering like balloons over toothpick necks and torsos.

'What do you think, they can't tell the kid isn't me?' whispered Estée. 'I mean, she doesn't look anything like me except her hair's the same color. Jesus.'

'All kids look alike,' said Bill, and then loudly, 'This is us in Yosemite, you see the geyser, what's it called . . .'

'Old Faithful?' piped up Unca Dicky.

'There you go,' said Bill. 'Now just a couple more.'

'This is a trip, they don't get it do they?' said Pete Magnus to Estée. 'What a trip, it's hilarious. Guy's got a real sense of humor.'

'Yeah,' said Estée. 'He's funny.'

'Here you see us at Disneyland,' said Bill. 'There's Esty next to Mickey there, you got your Goofy in the corner, summer of what, '85.'

'Great pic, I love it,' said Pete Magnus nervously.

'But it's a publicity photo for Disney,' said Estée. 'It's got the logo at the bottom.'

'Cracks me up,' said Pete Magnus. 'Good one, Bill.'

'Last but not least,' said Bill, 'you got your high school graduation photo, Esty with all her friends here,' and he clicked the slide wheel into its last image, a generic frame of a huge group of students, faces too small to be recognized, flinging mortarboards into the air.

Sporadic applause.

'What a beautiful childhood,' murmured Aunt Ruthie.

'You were lucky, you should appreciate,' said Uncle Jerry.

'Gave her everything she wanted,' piped up Aunt Sara, and Bill was Mr. Congeniality, beaming to beat the band.

'Now time for our special announcement,' he said. Two businessmen were still seated at the table, one bald, the other on crutches. From upstairs came sounds of breaking glass and gales of laughter, faint and musical, then strident. Feet thundered across the ceiling, bedsprings groaned. Betty had put down her inhaler and was smiling vacantly, nodding, hands in her lap. The old people played with food remnants and looked down at their plates.

'This is a special announcement,' Bill repeated. 'My daughter Esty here is getting married!'

Into the absentminded oohs of geriatrics Estée made her protest. 'What are you *talking* about?'

'With a generous dowry of over 100,000 shares in the Coca-Cola Company, she is betrothed to Mr. Pete Magnus, over here on the right.'

'Hey Bill, spring this on a guy,' joked Pete Magnus weakly, his voice trailing off.

'Ridiculous,' said Estée.

'I mean Bill, hey, we just only met,' said Pete Magnus, trying for good-natured ribbing. 'I mean hey, I'm not that kind of guy!'

'Here's the deal,' said Bill, leaning over to talk out of the side of his mouth. 'This stock, common, it's at, what, thirty-bucks a share, this is all yours if you get married to my daughter.'

'No way,' said Estée.

'Just look after her, put her up,' said Bill. 'Get married when you feel like it.'

'Forget it,' said Estée.

'Pete, is it a deal?' Bill handed him a leather portfolio across the tabletop.

'Sheesh, goddamn,' said Pete Magnus, an apologetic look at Estée, all the while opening the portfolio, pulling out a sheaf of stock certificates. 'Bill, never so shocked in my—'

'The young couple!' yelled Bill, straightening again.

'My daughter Esty and her new hubby Pete! Let's give
'em a hand!'

Applause started up, a pitter-patter of weak hand-
clapping from the relatives. One executive slapped his
knee, while the other stared at his watch.

'Just take it,' said Estée to Pete Magnus. 'I don't care.
No one's getting married.'

'Pete here,' said Bill, 'is gonna be my son-in-law!' He
leaned over the table and grabbed Pete Magnus by the
hand while Estée rolled her eyes. Betty clapped mechan-
ically. 'Start up the band, boys,' crowed Bill. 'Better than
a cash gift, direct transfer, no capital gains tax, ain't that
right Petey? Your basis here is pretty high—' and Estée
left the table, grabbing her wine glass as she went. As she
passed the gimp executive he muttered to his companion, 'Guy needs to get a sponsor, take him to some
meetings.'

The path to her bedroom, where the overnight bag and
the strongbox lay waiting, was fraught with voyeuristic
detail. Corners yielded flashes of intertwined limbs, discarded clothing, blurred, rapid movement. On the stairs
she passed the redhead, straddling a guest with his pants
down, and a golden square marked Trojan. Another man,
cradling a helium tank, recited, 'Hail Mary, full of grace,'
at high-pitched hysterical speed, and in the hallway
above, where she stopped at the telephone table to call
for a taxi, a limp brassiere adorned Betty's favorite hanging fern. Its owner crawled over to reclaim it with
wriggles and cries of 'You old horndog!' as her pursuer
attacked from behind. Naked save for a loosened tie, and
a face lipsticked onto his stomach with nipples for eyes,

he reared up on his knees and made his belly button talk by sucking his stomach in and pushing it out again. 'Hey babe, wanna ride in my car?' and the fern's pot crashed down, spilling soil on the carpet.

In her bedroom Estée interrupted a threesome, two girls jumping on the mattress in high-heeled shoes, observed by a man in one of Betty's wigs.

'Excuse me,' she said, and tried to reach under the bed, but her request went unheeded and the bed collapsed on her arm. The springs scratched and pricked and the jumping jacks tumbled downward, engulfing the dilapidated suit, who lay prone and gazing skyward. She grabbed her strongbox, dragged it out, scoring bloodlines into the skin of her arm, and was ready.

The redhead, blocking her exit path, was hanging out of an oversize shirt. 'Got a rubber?' she asked the jumping jacks. 'It broke, I only had one. I don't want that sheepskin crap. Plus I could use a Rolaid, you got one in your bag Tam?'

Estée made her way down the stairs again, where the redhead's john lay curled on the landing, grabbing at her foot as she passed. She shook him off.

'Esty!' said someone behind, and fearing interference from Bill she sprinted for the door. 'Wait a sec, shit. Hold on!'

Pete Magnus caught up with her on the front steps.

'Where you heading? Want a ride?'

'I called a taxi,' and she sat down to wait.

'Come on, I'll give you a ride, I'm going into L.A.,' urged Pete Magnus.

'That's okay.'

'I was wondering, is your father for real? This stock, I mean it's worth what, three million dollars, he's letting me walk off with it? I mean he seems kinda unstable, you know?'

'You were just a bystander,' said Estée.

'Let me drive you. Take forever to get in with a taxi. Where you headed? I live in the Hills, a condo. Drop you off anywhere. I mean this is the weirdest night of my life. You're talking hundreds for the taxi. You know the city?'

'I've never been. I always lived out here.'

'What never? And you're eighteen? You're what, an hour out here? Jesus. I mean Jesus. Poor little rich girl. You know?'

'I have a hotel.'

'No way, not letting you go by yourself, some sleazebag picks you up on the Strip, gets you on crack or horse or shit, makes you hook for a living, raw babe like you. I'm serious, dangerous out there. Come on.'

'You can just go,' she said, annoyed. 'I want to be alone.'

'Lemme get this straight,' he said, squatting on the stair. 'You're taking off because your folks are wacko, right? You on a budget? Because a taxi, that's gonna run you real money from here, I mean it. No one takes taxis in L.A. Especially not from out here in the boondocks. Let me drive you, drop you off wherever. You say the word. Okay?'

She ran over credits and debits in her head and rose reluctantly. 'You're not in this with him, are you? With my father?'

'A business deal, that's it,' said Pete Magnus. 'I hardly
know the guy.'

'You swear? You won't tell him where I am?'

'I swear,' said Pete Magnus. 'The buck stops here.'

She followed him to a parked convertible Mercedes
and slid into the passenger seat, the bag on her lap, arms
protecting it. She had to conserve her resources. It was a
new landscape and aid should not be scorned.

'Why are you in such a hurry, I mean what a great
setup,' said Pete Magnus, slamming his door and turning
the key. 'Crazy father handing out fortunes, I would stay
for the action, get a piece of it, Jesus shit, luckiest night of
my life!' he crowed, and rocked forward in his seat,
banging a fist on the steering wheel as they pulled out
onto the street. She turned and looked out the window at
the Kraft house receding into the distance.

'He paid to get rid of me,' said Estée. 'I was a Free Gift
with Every Purchase.'

'Hey now, shit,' said Pete Magnus. 'I don't know. No
idea the guy was so into me, model son-in-law material,
shit, barely know him. You know what it reminds me of?
Those kings and shit, that used to arrange marriages for
their kids. That's what it's like. Elevator doesn't go to
the top floor, though. Shit.'

She was silent, watching the neighborhood turn unfa-
miliar, feeling the leather of her seat.

'He tries to get it back, no legal way,' mused Pete
Magnus. 'No one has that much capital in a street
account, it's insane, hand over the paper like it was
Monopoly money. No fucking way. I give you ten to one
he realizes what he's done tomorrow, calls up, threats of

litigation, pressing charges, say I stole it out of his house, you don't give out that kind of money. Wacked. Calls my office tomorrow, lay money on it, shit.'

'Probably not,' said Estée.

'Goose that laid the golden egg,' said Pete Magnus, shaking his head as he steered them past an accident scene, two police cars flashing red and blue and a Datsun crushed into a guardrail, a mop of auburn hair against the steering wheel. 'Tries anything, we can talk turkey. Esty? You wanna help me out? I could help you too. We can help each other. You stay with me, sleep in the extra room, save money on the hotel?'

She said nothing. They were driving up an entrance ramp onto a freeway, moving at high speed, past a sign reading Interstate 10. West. She grabbed the sides of her seat. Cars zoomed by at frightening velocities, their tail-lights shrinking fast.

'That way I'll have a better conscience, see? I won't feel like I left you on your own. Just till we find you a place? I'll show you around. Help you get on your feet. Be great. How about it?'

'I don't know,' said Estée. He knew Bill. He might also be in league with the FBI men, with the police, all of whom were in collusion with Bill. He was driving fast and talking at the same time.

'You afraid of your dad? I mean I'm handling a lease-back situation for him, that's it, he knows my office number but he sure as hell doesn't know where I live, I'm not going to tell the guy where I live,' said Pete Magnus. 'A loose cannon. They can't find you, my home number's unlisted. It's a nice place, a penthouse, it's centrally

located, I can drive you for job interviews, give you a
hand? I mean it could be weeks till you find a decent
one-bedroom.'

'I don't know,' repeated Estée. There was nowhere to
put her eyes without them being dragged along, making
her dizzy, a burgeoning headache as she stared outward
to her right through the dark, at lighted digits on a tall
clock, billboards glowing from the trees. The moths had
refused to eat meat. They were used to plants. They
could not change.

'Specimen 76,' she murmured, 'could not adapt.'

'Say what?' said Pete Magnus.

There was no species known to her that had adapted
itself and then reversed its adaptation instantly when
the landscape changed. They died first. Maybe she
would starve without familiar food. She had always lived
in the house. Once Betty and Bill had been masses and
smells, had moved around her like shapes blotted by
light. It was when she got older that they had become
separate, identifiable, and remote, and a gap opened
between what they did and what she saw. She could still
remember, long ago, their warm arms. Had Bill brought
on the floods, reversed the laws of gravity, or had the cli-
mate changed after a natural disaster elsewhere, a cold
front moving in from far away? Betty's precedent was
lying down. She was emancipated from the need for
locomotion. She pretended satisfaction in her stasis,
though it reduced her slowly, cell by cell.

'You could even work for me, you know, like be a
temp,' said Pete Magnus. 'We need a good-looking recep-
tionist, what I have is this chick from the Valley, she

does her nails I swear to God, the stuff stinks, you can
smell it all over the office and she leaves like the trash
from her lunch right on the front desk. Whopper boxes,
fast food, greasy shit. It stinks to high heaven, which it's
no mystery how she put on the extra weight since all she
eats is this shit. She's just this stupid chick from Studio
City, I mean the accent puts people off. We could get rid
of her because she's late all the time so I can fire her
hassle-free, don't have to worry about lawsuits or whatever because I've already reprimanded her, she'd had the
warnings, shit I don't know how many times, she's actually skating on thin ice, I could bring you in, you can
type right? Use a computer, we're on IBM clones hooked
up to this database, pretty easy, and do phones, you'd
give the place a classy touch, plus which I'm thinking of
remodeling. Right now we've got this cheesy carpeting
practically looks like indoor-outdoor, I'm like ashamed to
bring clients in. I was going to go for a more modern
look, chrome and Lucite, this kinda high-tech look, go
ahead, make the outlay I know it'd be worth it, you could
like be part of the new look! I do a lot of phone business
and seriously you could add a kind of upscale feel, it's
like your dad's this hick from Hicksville though I'm not
saying he's completely in the dark businesswise, but how
you, I mean you talk like an educated person, you don't
talk like him at all, did you get it from your mom's side?
I mean, no offense, but you don't look like your dad, I
mean the guy's a mountain. It's amazing that someone
who looks like you could, like, be the fruit of his loom. I
mean he must hafta buy his clothes from Omar the Tent
Maker.'

They took an exit ramp and swerved to avoid a car making a left turn in front of them.

'Son of a bitch learn to fucking drive!' yelled Pete Magnus, and Estée looked down to inspect the phone, high-gloss black and compact, that lay in a console between them on the seat. 'I've been driving to my place, whaddaya think? Is it a deal?'

They pulled up at a crosswalk and waited for a staggering man to make his way across. A diamond-shaped sign next to the blinking orange hand, black letters on a yellow background, read Walk With Light.

part two

homo erectus

The penthouse was decorated in solid colors, expanses of cream-colored carpet, furniture of black brocade. It housed a collection of sculptures. 'African art,' explained Pete Magnus with a dismissive sweep of his hand. He had contacts, he reported, with an import-export consortium that brought the stuff in duty-free: fetishes of carved wood, totems, statues made of stone and clay. 'Primitive majesty, see. The noble savage and shit.' He indicated a spear-wielding wooden man squatting on the glass coffee table, ornamented with tufts of white animal hair. The wood man's face was bone-thin, his polished cheekbones gaunt on a long, sharp skull. Emaciated, leering, teeth filed down to sharp points, he was impervious to the man of the house, who patted the top of his head with patronly affection.

Pete folded down a sofabed in his spare room and brought out a pile of striped sheets, keeping up a patter on Virtuous Living. He was confident in his advice. 'You gotta be able to shift personal gears under stress,' he said. 'Maximize your potential. You gotta have drive, but you also gotta be able to relax.' On his desk Estée found a ballpoint pen that featured a girl in a white bikini. When

she turned it upside down the girl went naked. Watching
nervously as he swept a pile of magazines into a drawer,
she felt the viral tree of taxonomy take root, in whose
lower branches Pete dwelt, in congress with his brethren,
arboreal primates, among the gibbons and the siamangs,
whom evolution had favored with a median position.

'You sleep tight,' he said. 'Don't let the bedbugs bite.'

He did not close the door behind him. She could stay
where she was or she could move. She opened the window and breathed in the dark air. Lights dappling the
black land like stars, but the stars were invisible. Passage
was unconstrained, motion was unregulated. There were
countless options, all mysteries. She was stunned, let
loose, she was floating in a pool of the real. She was
unanchored. It was sink or swim. This had to be normal.
Normal had no directions. It was aimless. You struck out
along a path for no reason except to be moving. She
would have to arm herself against chance, against its
infinity. Position herself. Put her feet on dry land. The
liquid of choice might rush, rear up in massive tides,
swamp her and drown her. She took out her notebook
and wrote with the nude girl.

GLOSSARY: HOMO SAPIENS
Specimen 1: Real Estate Agent, Male.
Description: Puffy. Poor camouflage.
Habitat: Urban nest builder.
Behavior: Obstreperous. Aggression in male.
Diet: Carnivorous. Esp. Beef & Bean Burrito.

Already there was comfort in her command of the

situation. She had tools; she was trained in scientific method. She would make observations, record her findings, and build up a database. Then she could decide on an approach. 'Cover yourself,' she told the naked girl sternly, and flipped her. Burrowing into the sheets she flicked off the bedside lamp. She was a stowaway, she had to pass herself off as one of them. The task was monumental. From the living room she could hear Pete Magnus talking. 'I'm not kidding, I'm not kidding,' he said over and over. She got up to close her door, peeked around the jamb to see him leaning over his coffee table as he cradled a cordless phone on his shoulder. He sniffed at something on the table – salt? – and rubbed his nose, jabbering to the telephone. 'I swear to fucking God. It's like the goddamn lottery!'

She shut the door and went back to the bed, where, head on the cool pillow, she ascended the back of the great white bird and belted herself in. Something beefy and pink, in a halo, hovered over her. An angel pig?

'Left a key on the table,' it said. 'Come and go, do what you want. Eggos in the freezer. Make yourself at home. I gotta go in to the office.'

She sat up and blinked, but he was already out the door.

The street was loud and all made of stores. She was a tourist: she needed information. She asked a grocery store employee if he could answer some questions, but he was too busy piling oranges into a pyramid. She tried out lipsticks at Beauty Supply and was told to buy them or put them down. In the drugstore she saw endless combinations and permutations. The product categories were

distinct but within each category little variation was
allowed. Coty Airspun Powder-essence Liquid-Matte
Makeup, Ivory Silk, was identical to its nearest neighbors.
She made a note of it.

OBSERVATION 1: HOMO SAPIENS

The choices go on forever, but they are all the same.

She passed a video store, sporting goods, Allstate
Insurance. Everywhere the array of items was spectacular: even Betty's vast personal collection was dwarfed by
comparison. Jenny Craig, haircuts, greeting cards, compact discs. Then specialty clothing, dangling spiders, a
skull in the window, a dark interior. Inside she saw they
carried black shining synthetic apparel, chains, whips,
collars studded with pointy metal. In a display case were
surprising items labeled Locking Penis Chastity and
Patent Leather Bondage Mask. Her inquiries were met
with distaste. Questions large in scope were not toler-
ated. Discussion had to be practical, minute, and
succinct. Obviously they didn't like tourists. There were
no guides available.

At the end of the afternoon, after a Coca-Cola from a
machine, she returned to the apartment. Pete Magnus,
clad in wraparound towel, was on the telephone again.
He pushed a button and put the phone down.

'Wanna go out? Drinks with some guys. Friend Stew,
he's in advertising. They don't card at this place. C'mon,
it'll be good for you.'

The place was full of people milling and holding glasses.
Their short-term goals were unclear. Luckily she had

science on her side, and science was hypothesis testing. But before she could test the hypothesis, she had to have one. Observation was the only way: look, listen, learn. Bill had said it himself. Conversations were circular, like animals chasing their tails: their purpose appeared to be affirmation. The male code, disguised as idle chatter about sports teams and their activities, was unbreakable. She escaped to the restroom at intervals to record her findings.

GLOSSARY: HOMO SAPIENS
Specimen 2: Advertising Assistant, Male.
Description: Weasel face. Tropical plumage.
Behavior: Insecure around dominant males. Vies for position by squawking.
Diet: "I'll have machos with cheese."

When Pete Magnus took Stew aside and whispered to him, Stew threw his arms out and whooped, spilling the mush of a daiquiri on a woman behind him. 'Who cares? Hey lady, Petey here can buy you a whole new outfit, shit! You kidding? No way man. You serious?' After that Stew concentrated on Estée. He sat close in the booth, his shoulder against hers. A Stew hand brushed against her knee. She listened to the tale of his marital breakup. It became clear that Stew was targeting her, Estée, for possible fertilization. But she was prepared. She knew what it had done to Betty.

Specimen 2: Advertising Assistant, Male.
Addendum
Mating Habits: Competitive; promiscuous. Biological

imperative: distribute semen to multiple females. Does
not mate for life.
Objective: Mass insemination.

Stew was a quick study. 'We're married for like three
months and she's going, I need time, I'm not comfortable
with my body, and this kind of crap. Plus which she had
this friend she was always talking to with the door
closed, the woman I know for sure is a dyke. I mean it
sure as hell wasn't me, know what I mean?' Drawing
near for confessions, breathing close to her face, Stew
attempted to encroach on the area surrounding her person. Feeling that outright rejection of Stew would result
in verbal recriminations and abuse, Estée was able to
forestall these effects by gently caressing Stew with
Stew-affirming rhetoric, while quietly though firmly dis-
abusing Stew of the notion that she would like to be
inseminated by him.

And then Pete Magnus bore down again, and the onus
of persuasion was no longer upon her. She was clear of
the first hurdle. She was learning the vernacular.

Afterward she let herself be transported back to the
apartment, numb with overload in the passenger seat.
The night street was a shifting swarm of cars, metal and
rubber and glass in parallel migration. The drivers alongside Pete Magnus's car knew where they were going.
They had plans. Their eyes contained maps of the city.
They were supercomputers, data banks of endless coded
digits with no overt meaning. She was only a receiver.
She received signals. It was too soon to process them.

Over additional beers in the living room, remote

control in hand, Pete Magnus told her what her expenses would be if she lived by herself. 'You gotcher rent, first off, then utilities, your gas, electric and your phone, plus a water bill maybe. Then you got health insurance, your dental, plus you gotta have a car in L.A. You gotta get insurance for liability, the minimum's like $25,000 for uninsured motorists. Then you gotcher furniture, you need kitchen appliances – shit, did you see that? What a kick, goddamnit. Esty? Would you be a pal and get me another Wicked Ale?'

'I can't drive,' said Estée, in awe.

'You got no license? Eighteen and no license?'

'He didn't want me to drive.'

'This is bad,' he said. 'No car in L.A., you're a cripple. They might as well hack off your legs.'

'All those things you said, do I have to pay for them? What if I don't want them?'

'Stop yanking my chain,' said Pete Magnus.

'But I don't want them, all I need is to be somewhere.'

'You can't just be somewhere,' he said. 'You gotta pay for it. You pay for everything Esty. Heat, cold, a bed, all that shit Esty. When you left your parents' house there you gave up your free ride. Babe in the woods. I mean literally. Wake-up call. Everything has a price. A free good in this world Esty, a free good is a good with no value. Something's free, it means no one will pay money for it. Means it sucks Esty. Remember that.'

'But just to be somewhere? It costs money?'

OBSERVATION 2: HOMO SAPIENS

There is a tariff for being alive.

'Shit,' said Pete Magnus, 'it goes without saying. Most natural thing in the world. Gotcher resources, right? Then you got demand, you got free enterprise, Adam Smith, wealth of nations, gotcher highest bidder your lowest seller and bingo.'

'Who's Adam Smith?' asked Estée.

'Some guy in business school, made these videos about I forget exactly what, maybe how to be a self-starter or like the difference between tax avoidance and evasion. Video called *Wealth of Nations* they showed us. Anyway, my point is you gotta get there first. The three elements are timing, speed, and vision. Like I'll see a property and I'll jump onto it, oftentimes I find out the next day I beat another guy out by a hair. A hair's *breath*.' He muted a commercial and changed channels, settling on basketball highlights played to the droning voice of a commentator. She got up to get him the beer and one for herself.

In Bill's house she had taken objects for granted. Clearly their apparent willingness to serve had been deceptive. In the new world she was unowned, but also owned nothing. There was a link. No good to ask Pete Magnus. His efforts were wholly directed toward expansion. She was interested in subsistence.

'Way it works, one guy sees the other guy needs something, so he makes it for him, that is if he has what we call comparative advantage, Esty. That's when the opportunity cost of producing something is less than what it costs to buy it. Gotcher tradeoff ratios, your production possibility curves, all that shit Esty. Comparative advantage. If you're lucky Esty, you got what we call absolute advantage. *Ab-so-lute* advantage. That's when you got something no one else got. What you gotta do, you trade your labor in for money, spend the money on buying things. You turn time into goods Esty. It's like magic.'

Even the air had become commodified, every segment of the earth apportioned off to an entrepreneur. There was no plot of land anywhere not laid claim to by a number, not described by other numbers, kidnapped and held for ransom to anyone whose hapless body, with dimensions and wants far beyond its control, chanced to rest on its surface. The earth was a grid, subdivided by owner.

'Shit, this isn't cold. Fuckin warm beer, make me sick.'

'I don't like that,' she said. 'Time into goods.'

'Surprised your dad didn't tell you about business. It's like the only thing that guy's not wacked about. He knows business, Esty. What did he talk about all your life? I mean, Christ. Didn't you go to school?'

'I did before,' she said, 'but then he took me out.'

'Jesus Esty. Fuckin weird.'

'I brought some things to sell,' she said. 'Jewelry and stuff.'

'Jewelry, that won't keep you in socks Esty. You better stay with me. We'll figure out something. I'll show you the ropes Esty. Teach you some skills. Found out those shares are for real, he bought 'em through his broker and convened them to street. Don't think I'm not grateful Esty. You stick with me.'

In the morning she watched from her window and continued to take notes.

GLOSSARY: HOMO SAPIENS
Specimen 3: U.S. Postal Worker, Male.
Description: Nonvenomous.
Further observation needed.

Then she watched television. It was a vast empire and educational too, but she had to stop taking notes. She let the deluge come. She stared at it for hours and tried to distinguish its categories, but they were indistinct. At 4:12 by the digital clock on the VCR the doorbell rang and she answered it eagerly, notebook in hand. Two men were there, a tall bug-eyed one in a suit, a short one in a T-shirt that pictured a dove. Caution must be exercised.

'Do you have a minute, one minute in your busy day to spare for news that could change your life?' said the shorter man. He was sweating.

'I have minutes,' she said.

'We want t-to ask you,' said the tall man. He ran a finger along the inside rim of his collar and looked to the short man, who nodded encouragement. 'We want to ask you, have y-y-you ak-ak-ak-ak—' He broke off, clenching his fists.

'Go Ron,' said the short man, and patted the other on the back. 'Doing real well, Ron.'

'Ak-ak-ak—'

'You can do it, Ron.'

'—ak-cepted Jesus Christ as your p-p-personal savior?'

'Great Ron. Perfect.'

'Does it cost money?'

'The Lord comes fr-fr-freely to His children.'

'Because the jewelry won't keep me in socks.'

'May we come in?' asked the short man. 'It's the heat.'

'Sure,' she said, and led them to Pete Magnus's couch. Here, already, was evidence that Pete Magnus's information was inaccurate. No money was required for Jesus. They sat down beside each other, leaning forward together. Ron took out a handkerchief and wiped his face.

'Are you aware,' said the short man, 'that Jesus said, "I am the way, the truth, and the life: no man cometh unto the Father, but by me"?'

'No.'

'John 14:6,' said the short man. 'In Corinthians, it is said, "Be not deceived: neither fornicators, nor idolaters, nor adulterers, nor effeminate, nor abusers of themselves with mankind shall inherit the kingdom of God." Would you happen to have a glass of water for my friend here? I think he's dehydrated.'

'What the hell is this?' said Pete Magnus from the doorway.

'Jesus Christ,' said Estée. 'It's free.'

'Up you get,' said Pete Magnus, dropping his briefcase. 'Get out, guys. Out!'

'I was just going to get a glass of water for Ron,' said Estée.

'Sir,' said Ron, rising on unsteady legs, his hands trembling, 'have you ak-ak-ak—?'

'What is this, dysfunctional Jews for Jesus? Get out already, go save some other loser. There's a guy who needs your help on the third floor. He's going to male empowerment therapy. No sweat, I'll waive the referral fee. Just get outta here buddy. I mean it.'

'—ak-ak-ak—'

'Eat me,' said Pete Magnus, and shoved the short man out after Ron. He slammed the door behind them.

'But it was free,' said Estée. 'You said nothing was free.'

'Esty,' said Pete Magnus, shaking his head, 'that shit is for losers, okay? Losers. You can't be letting Jesus freaks in here. They'll talk your ear off and leave you with bull-shit. What did I tell you, Esty? If something's for free, you don't want it. Lesson Number One. Someone offers you something free, you say no. Because what that means is they couldn't sell it if they tried. You got that?'

Annoyed, she held her notebook tight against her and headed for her room. He had interfered with her research.

'Listen Esty, you're lonely. I understand. I'll introduce you to some people. No problem. Hey, you know how to cook?'

GLOSSARY: HOMO SAPIENS

Specimen 4: Jesus Freak, Male.
Description: Rigid. Bulging eyes.
Behavior: Free samples. No obligation.

That night Pete Magnus took her to another bar for margaritas and introduced her to Dave, Specimen 5, CPA, and Rick, Specimen 6, Data Systems Consultant. But it was Stew who broke the camel's back. It happened while he was discoursing to Estée on the subject of a surgical procedure undergone by his brother.

'They make these incisions, right,' he said, with his

hand on the back of her bar stool, encroaching, 'and put these inflatable pumps in the guy's dick. So he like presses a button on his balls, I'm not kidding, and the thing inflates like a balloon. There's this saltwater they shoot in you. Saline solution or whatever. For ten thousand bucks.' He was staring over her shoulder. 'Christ, it's Lee Ann. That bitch! I can't believe she's here. My ex just came in.' Estée turned and followed his gaze. She saw a bouffant woman in pink on the arm of a bodybuilder.

Pete Magnus was submerged in a crowd of rowdy sports fans in front of a wide-screen monitor; Dave had struggled off to the bathroom saying, 'I'm gonna chuck.' Estée was stranded and had no time to protest when Stew kidnapped her and towed her to the table where his ex-wife and the weightlifter were sitting. Stew had bought five drinks already and was working on his sixth. Burping, he clenched his hand to Estée's waist and announced she was his girlfriend.

'Little young, Stew,' said his wife, and turned away as the Neanderthal ridge on the weightlifter's brow furrowed in suspicion. Estée smiled weakly and tried to twist out of Stew's grasp.

'Who's the pinhead?' asked Stew. His wife ignored him. The bodybuilder stood, said his name was Larry, and asked Stew to remove himself from the vicinity. 'Fuck you,' said Stew.

'Look buddy,' said the bodybuilder, 'we're just looking for a nice, quiet drink. So don't get in my face.'

'What, celebrating?' asked Stew.

'It's our four-month anniversary,' said Lee Ann, and patted the bodybuilder's bicep.

'Of what, the first fuck?' asked Stew, and posited the theory that Lee Ann and Larry had resorted to canine approaches to sexual activity, due to the crops of steroid-induced acne on Larry's person – acne that, in Stew's view, would prove repulsive to Lee Ann in the event of full-frontal intercourse. Estée turned her back and watched the crowd at the bar. Larry threatened physical harm. Stew responded by punching him. It was a weak, misplaced left hook that glanced off Larry's shoulder, but Lee Ann emitted a high whine of protest. Estée tried to step back, but Stew grabbed her and forced her in front of him as Larry's fist descended in a roundhouse right. It caught her on the side of the head, crashing her to the ground.

Larry bent over her. 'You okay?' A film of water blurred her eyesight, but she could see Stew launch a new attack against the bodybuilder, and Dave and Pete Magnus entered the fray. Estée could not get up. She was afraid one of her back molars was loose, felt a cold bitter wetness in her throat, warm liquid coursing from her nose. Someone kicked her in the ribs and she doubled over, gasping, trying to pull herself underneath the nearest table, grabbing at a woman's leg. The leg kicked her hand away and then burrowed its toes into her abdomen, drilling there relentlessly until the table fell over, crushing Estée's ankle. Someone landed hard on her hip, next a hard weight on her head, and she covered her face with her hands, her cheek ground against the gritty floor.

She saw and tasted brown; the air was muddy. Stew and Larry were strange Visigoths from the Discovery Channel, pillagers, rapists. Their legs were tree trunks, their brains were acorns. Cudgels studded with metal swung above her head amidst the roars of the victors and the screams of the vanquished. She felt an elbow grind into her temple and then release. She was hoisted onto her feet and dragged, the night air was on her face. She blinked tears from her eyes and licked at the salty blood around her mouth; her neck ached too much for her to raise her head or turn, so she saw only two pairs of columnar legs ascending, khaki pants and denim.

Behind them, imprecations and warnings were hurled; feminine voices screeched rebuke; Pete Magnus leaned down beneath her face as she was jogged along. 'Esty? You okay?' He had a cut of his own on the cheek, was red-faced and breathing hard. His hair was matted with sweat.

They opened the back door of Pete Magnus's car and helped her in, and she collapsed sideways across the leather seats. Someone propped her head up on a rolled towel. The top of the Mercedes was down and she welcomed the bite of fresh oxygen. She felt warm blood from her nose. The car doors slammed and they were rolling. She was a loose bundle of nerves rattled by the jagged stops and starts, scalp abraded by stiff fibers of terry cloth. There was a hot spot on the top of her head and she was airy, watching the faint stars pass above them, the lights of a plane coming in to land. It was a ship in air, a chariot of fire. She was sailing. It was a black sea like velvet, like luxury.

'Th'fuck were you thinking?'

'Gimme a break. I'm, let me over I'm gonna puke.'

'Petey, case in point. He's shitfaced. Not his fault.'

'Emergency room?'

'Just slap a bag of ice on there shit.'

'Pull in there, the liquor store, buy some ice.'

'She's not a baby. Just a concussion'

'No big deal.'

'—brain damage or shit? Huh Stew? . . . the hell was she involved? She's eighteen years old, she's lived in like seclusion, now this? A brain-damaged chick? Fat fucking lawsuit?'

She relaxed her efforts at listening and faded into the upholstery, her hands in fists beneath her chin, shivering from the breeze.

In her bedroom at Pete Magnus's they applied an ice pack to the side of her head. She lay in bed and heard them squabbling as they sat there, subjects as diverse as the game, the fight, Stew's ex, Larry's zits, a multilevel home Pete had sold for $2.3 million, a Nike slogan, 'just do it.' She couldn't find the side of her head. 'Hello, excuse me,' she said to Pete Magnus, but they ignored her feeble quaver from their huddle on the Naugahyde love seat.

'Subdural hematoma,' said the nurse. A man in a lab coat leaned down and pricked her arm. 'Whoever was responsible for the ice pack caused clotting. Could have been a fatal error. You're lucky mister.' Were they experimenting on her? Above them, white; directly in front, a television slanting from the ceiling. Pete Magnus, in his business attire, bent down to explain.

'You were in a coma for eight days,' said Pete Magnus. His shirt changed from yellow to green and his breath was garlicky. 'It was a kind of blood clot,' consoled the doctor. 'Cut off the circulation to the brain. You made a remarkable recovery and we're all *very proud*. You're fine now.'

'I'm fine now,' repeated Estée.

Pete Magnus said something else, but she was unable to concentrate. When he left, an old, bald man was standing there in a light-blue gown. He leaned over and poked her breast with a finger, laughed *hee hee hee*, and tottered away. The gown was open in the back to expose the crack of his buttocks and a forest of gray hair therein.

She did not have a clock in her room and, frequently sedated, was at a loss to understand time passing. There were more visits from Pete Magnus. He brought her flowers, silver balloons, bright, glossy magazines called *People* and *Us*, and a Godiva box of chocolates, which the old man stole and ate in fifteen minutes. He stood beside her bed, staring at her for hours, and rambled about his wife. His wife was a kleptomaniac, but dead.

Orderlies brought food to her on plastic trays, consisting mainly of puddings, soups, and cold meat she let the old man steal. A miscalculation had brought her to this pass. Was it her fault? She clung to scientific method. Even in the hospital, research must continue. Her system was in its infancy, but it would mature. If you're going to do something, do it right, said Bill.

GLOSSARY: HOMO SAPIENS

Specimen 7: Old Man.

Description: Wrinkly, odorous, scaly. Removable teeth.

Reptilian subspecies?

Habitat: Hospital.

Behavior: Preys on disabled females. Hides remote
control. Guards jealously.
Diet: Scavenger.

Specimen 8: Registered Nurse.
Description: Large.

Walking was slow and made her head hurt. She began
to make short trips at night, after visiting hours, when the
corridors were empty and she was free to enter the rooms
of other patients for the purpose of gathering data. One
night they rolled a second patient into her room, a woman
on a gurney. She was labeled Helen on the chart at the end
of her bed. Her husband sat with her during visiting hours.
He wore glasses and was quiet, but Helen was talkative.
She told Estée she was having an operation.

GLOSSARY: HOMO SAPIENS

Specimen 12: Helen.
Description: Hollow face, thin.
Habitat: Photographs of infant. Wall decorated with quo-
tations. 'Greater love hath no man.'
Behavior: Nonaggressive.
Remarks: 'He's three. I'm the only match we have, he
needs my bone marrow. He's sick.'

The night before the operation, Estée was woken by
noises. The husband and Helen were lying together on
top of the sheets. Her legs were smooth and clean as
bones, her fingers splayed on the back of the husband.
She was crying and smiling, her head and shoulders

moving up and down in steady rhythm. Estée turned away and looked at the wall, which was gray in the dark, but then she looked back.

'Oh Helen,' said the husband, and then his voice caught and his legs went stiff.

'Don't worry,' said Helen quietly. Her face was silver. She looked over and Estée was afraid she saw her watching, but she kept on smiling. Inside her eyes she was old. 'Don't worry,' she repeated, looking at Estée over the husband's head. 'The future is bright.'

Estée, itchy with shame, shut her eyes and hid her face in the pillow. In the morning Helen was not in her bed. After lunch they did not bring her back. When the sun was setting and the bed marked 'Helen' was still bare, Estée padded down, in her bare feet, to the nursing station.

'She will not be returning to the room,' said the big nurse, and shut her lips tight.

'Is she fine?' asked Estée.

The nurse turned away and shuffled papers on a chart. Later, in the night again, the husband came in. He took the quotations off the wall and the clothes from the stand beside the bed. He picked up the picture of Helen's baby and put it in a bag. He was quiet. Estée sat up in her bed.

'Is she fine?' she asked him.

'No,' he said. 'She is not fine. She is gone.'

Then he left.

GLOSSARY: HOMO SAPIENS

Specimen 12:

Gone.

She was flossing her teeth – the back molar loosened during the brawl had been extracted and her tongue played, with some melancholia, in its warm little hole – when she looked up to the medicine-cabinet mirror and was shocked to behold the corpulent and evil physiognomy of Bill.

She sat down on the tile floor, which smelled of lemon-scent disinfectant. All formal observations of the species must be shelved. She had her father's eyes, but not his fat arms or legs, which took up the space of others. His system was deficient.

She got up and leaned on the sink, and in this position spent two hours staring at her reflection, until at long last Bill's tiny swine eyes disappeared into her own, his upturned snout shrank back into the contours of her nose, and his triple chin receded and vanished. He bowed out of her, genuflecting as he retreated, and seeped dark and wraithlike into the toilet tank. But her innocuous reflection was only the skin: beneath it her veins and organs swelled with hereditary toxins. She would expunge them by sheer force of will.

They discharged her in the afternoon. An orderly wheeled her out in a chair, as per hospital policy, with Pete Magnus walking alongside. She was dizzy but otherwise whole.

'Kept your room for you Esty,' said Pete Magnus. 'Your bag, your stuff, kept it all safe and sound.'

While he was at work she counted her money, put Betty's jewels into a plastic Vons bag, and boarded a Rapid Transit vehicle going to Wilshire Boulevard, where Collateral Lenders of Beverly Hills was located. She left the jewels to be appraised, ate lunch reading *People*, and went back to pick them up.

'Not even your expensive imitations, your cheap paste is what these here are,' said the man behind the counter, and dangled the supposed Cartier bracelet from a forefinger as though it were a carrier of buboes.

Sickened, knees weak, she stuffed the maligned trinkets into her bag and slouched out of the store. The pawnshop man and Pete Magnus were nothing but bearers of bad tidings. They were the salesmen of the normal, and they were everywhere. She had to make an odyssey. The risk factor was slight, for the Krafts could not capture her and keep her at home now. Those days were past. Bill had given Pete Magnus a lot of money; it was possible that he would consent to give her something. Not probable, but possible. She studied the bus routes, left a Post-it note for Pete Magnus on the refrigerator, and struck out for Santa Monica Boulevard.

By the time she got to her old neighborhood it was twilight. Tall palm trees with tiny heads swayed in the breeze, and as she made her way along the sidewalk to the cul-de-sac a streetlight winked out. But she saw, and stood still in her tracks. There was no house. The lot was empty. Where the Kraft residence had stood there was only bare ground.

She wandered through the gate, the iron gate inscribed with a flowing capital *K*, past a blackened patch of grass where the customs booth had been, up the crescent drive, still extant. There was the line of trees ahead that had formed the back boundary between Kraft and the neighboring gardens; there was the burial mound for the roosters, the same earth she remembered, and the square lot of sand and gravel that had served as their forum. Nothing else. The lawn was scorched in the configuration of the house's blueprint. Ashes had been cleared, debris, every component, brace, beam, foundation stone, cinder block, everything was gone. Even the basement had been filled in: fresh dirt was level with the burned ground. She dragged her foot along the dead grass and heard it rustle like old paper – desiccated, brittle.

She wandered around the perimeter of the lawn once, twice, and then went out the gate again, walked slowly back to the bus stop and waited.

'Burned to the ground?' said Pete Magnus, chewing on a carrot. 'What happened? Who can you ask? There was nothing in the news. Don't you know your old neighbors, or like friends of the family?'

'The family has no friends,' said Estée, but then she remembered the crematorium. They would know where Bill was and what had happened to Kraft.

'Bill Kraft? With a K? Never heard of him,' said the manager heartily behind the echo of his speakerphone.

'But he owns the place,' said Estée. 'He's my father.'

'Owned by a Dallas-based conglomerate, give you their number for verification if you like,' said the manager.

She hung up. 'Lawyer?' queried Pete Magnus. 'Or maybe they were in the obits if they, like, if they were in the house at the time?'

Research proved fruitless. Giving up on her cycles of phone calls to newspapers, to Information in Akron, Detroit, and St. Louis, where Betty's maiden name yielded only dead ends, relinquishing her round of field trips to reference libraries where she perused local papers, obituary columns for two counties under which K gave forth Konditsiotis, Marlie, 74, Keger, James, 76, Kantry, Emma, 65, and Kreet, Bernice, 43, she took it upon herself to retire to the sofabed, where she stayed for three days. She moved and flailed her arms in restless, semiconstant sleep through dreams of Bill in flames, his blubber burning orange like a whale-oil lamp.

If Bill had come full circle to the end, it stood to reason he had seen at last that he and Betty were specimens too, had chosen as his final form pyromaniac and ignited his own habitat. Once he made this final judgment, to which all other judgments had led, he might have watched as Betty shrank where she lay, grew softly dead as wisps of smoke trailed through the rosebud lips of a shining plastic Boop mask.

Until Pete Magnus, refusing to take no for an answer, roused her and propelled her out into the kitchen, there to feed her milk, toast, and pep. She was healthy again, he reminded her, though on the side of her head were contusions; yellow bruises climbed along her ribs, thighs, and shins, and she felt a twinge in her hip when she twisted from the waist. She should count herself lucky.

'Come on Esty,' said Pete Magnus. 'Gotta move on, put it behind you. Hard to accept, you're depressed, I'm here to help. They're probably just on vacation or something, sold the house to developers, putting up like a golf course or condos there so they tore the place down. Relocating, you know, kids leave and the old folks need a smaller place, I see it all the time. They'll be in touch.

Stressed about money? Stay here. What's mine is yours, babe. Just don't be so depressed, you gotta get out more. Boys miss you, Stew goes, Where's that babe Esty, he's all, What's up with her, and I go, She'll be back Stew, right? Just an accident, she won't hold it against you guys. I go, she'll be fine. She's a survivor.'

GLOSSARY

FINAL ENTRY

Prognosis for Specimen 1, Real Estate Agent:
Extinction

t w o

Pete Magnus announced a scheme to broker the site of an Arizona nursing home to a strip-mining outfit. Overnight he shifted into high gear. He brought his work home with him and spent the mornings talking on his cordless phone while Estée brewed coffee and toasted bread. Between calls he stuffed his mouth and confided in her his workaday trials.

'Marsha, right, this woman that works for me? She's irritating the hell out of me. She's doing this primal scream therapy, she chants a lot and she has this altar set up in her filing cabinet. Her husband won't let her do it at home so she's doing it at the office, and I mean she locks the door and shit but there I am on the speakerphone and through the wall she's chanting oogala boogala.'

'Primal scream?' asked Estée, pouring orange juice.

'You don't do the scream right away, you have to work up to it. She's been in this therapy for a year or something, she still hasn't worked up to the scream, all she does is fucking chant. Come in at the wrong time and she's cross-legged in front of the filing cabinet with her eyes closed going oogala boogala schmoogala doogala.'

'Eggs?'

'Awright, take 'em off your hands. Gonna think big from now on, Esty. Been playing it safe but now I'm going big, big, big. What's that asshole's number, my asshole broker, guy's got a corncob up his ass. Steve? Strategy here, I wanna offload all the blue-chip, total liquidation as soon as it's up say three-eighths on the Argentine ITT, a quarter with the Coca-Cola. Esty, hand me the half-and-half wouldja?'

She left the kitchen, taking her toast into the living room to eat in front of Joan Lunden's 'Good Morning' face. Padding into the hall where her closet was to look for a pair of underwear, she burrowed in the dirty clothes hamper and, scrabbling through the soiled mass of Pete Magnus's king-size sheets, found a fifty-dollar bill in his pants. She pocketed it slyly.

Sitting on the side of his bed, Pete donned lozenged socks while holding the receiver couched between his jaw and collarbone.

'What are you talking about, buying-selling like crazy, make a big fat fucking commission, what do you even care if I crap on myself? But I won't, Steve, I won't I gotta feeling. Steve, you're lucky I don't take my business to a deep discount house, trade at two cents a share, save myself your goddamn fat-cat cut,' and he waved a shoe at Estée, bidding her to forage for its mate in the pile on the floor. 'What do you mean I don't know, capital gains bullshit, turn it over, but listen I gotta go. That's why I said three, I figured in the IRS levy, at this point I just need liquid, whaddaya think, no, I gotta go, catch ya later Steve,' and he hung up and joined Estée in scrounging around for the shoe.

'Seizing the fuckin day,' he told her. 'Been lying in wait, all these assets sitting there, I mean shit I'm taking risks, gonna go for broke, why stay small? You ever hear that song by that purple midget Prince, you know Ronnie's got a bomb we could all die any day, you seen my Filofax?' and then, while in the background she tore his Porsche calendar off the wall of her bedroom, he was dialing again. 'I tolja already when we signed the lease-back deal it was — the lease runs out in July, so what I think we gotta sell the property, gotta crazy offer from this company in Tulsa, keep it quiet obviously,' and she crumpled the calendar into a waste can, opened desk drawers and scanned their contents. The stack of magazines pertaining to his apartment, named *Penthouse*, she removed. Flipping through one she saw its subject matter was not real estate. 'What are you telling me, give me this grandmother shit? No, if it was my grandmother I'd go honey, time to move on. What two hundred seniors? Give me this Golden Age crap. Move 'em out! Outside Tucson there it's geriatric heaven, they got your dude ranches look like the Taj Ma-fuckin-hal, there's a godzillion nursing homes, it's like a Disneyland for dialysis machines. Please, relocation's not gonna kill 'em.'

'Pete?' she asked, walking into his bedroom. He was rubbing a Mennen Speed Stick on his armpits. 'I'm cleaning my room. Do you need these magazines?'

'Christ,' he said, and dropped them in a corner.

'Onanism is healthy,' recited Estée. 'It's really the best way. When you're older I will show you the devices.'

'What?' he asked, distracted, but before she could

repeat Betty's dictum he had knotted his tie and was on his way out.

He upped his rate of acquisition of native art, bringing home a despoiled icon almost every day: now a Fon iron statue, now a Baule figurine; Monday a Makishi dancer costume, Tuesday a Dukduk mask. Pete was on a spending quest. He bought luxury foodstuffs wholesale, storing cartons of capers and anchovy paste in the broom closet, crates of Belgian chocolate in the bathroom. In a flurry of extravagance he purchased a huge truck on jacked-up wheels, which he equipped with a booming stereo system. 'I'll teach you to drive Esty, get around on your own.' He no longer troubled himself to turn off faucets, burners, or fans; water ran constantly, sometimes from multiple taps at once while Estée went around shutting them off. He often switched on the heater to counteract the effects of the air conditioner. The laundry went unwashed until Estée put it in the washing machine. He left cartons of milk going sour on the counter, broken beer bottles on the kitchen linoleum.

She told herself that, being an unpaying guest, she could set no conditions to her tenancy, and it was natural that, while he was trying to get big, mundane events were beneath him. The world was now, he told Estée, his oyster. Apparently he was a pearl, swimming in gray mollusk muscle. A pearl did not concern itself with its oyster, though the oyster built itself around the pearl.

Pete Magnus's burgeoning mass was filling the finite space of the apartment. If she was uncomfortable with overlap she would have to shrink to accommodate, contract as he expanded. To this end she did not respond to his displays and was stiff and unforthcoming in mixed company. She avoided Stew and company. The form her shrinking took was covert: she kept exchanges to a minimum, made no demands, and receded quietly under verbal assault. Her situation, she assumed, was of brief duration, peopled by temporary characters and governed by arbitrary rules. Bearing with it was less a function of stoicism than of cost-effectiveness. She had to acclimatize. Advances were incremental: the real grew at her sides in the shape of new wings, vestigial and membranous. She loitered in public places, waiting to learn. It would happen by accretion, like geology. But Pete Magnus was not a patient man.

'What you gotta have, Esty, is people skills,' he urged. 'You gotta be able to make people do what you want. You're not gonna learn that at the library Esty. I mean you're a good-looking girl, you could be a model or something. You just gotta know how to work it. Keep it in mind Esty. When you get up in the morning, say to yourself: people skills. Aims, goals, and objectives. Interaction. You're too quiet Esty. What people like most about me is, why I sell so many houses is, I can talk Esty. I have what you call conversational flair. Take it from me. Every morning I get up, I take a look in the mirror, and I go, Pete, today is going to be a great day. And why? Because I got aims, I got goals, I got objectives.'

She schooled herself in Magnus appreciation. She conjugated verbs on his behalf: like, likes, likability. I like Pete. Pete is neat.

Tiring of boring old Nigerian bronzes, Pende masks, and Sri Lankan disease-devil faces, he brought home the

pièce de résistance one Friday night. He announced a
celebration, with delivery food to come. He had an elec-
trician wire a light into the wall and bolted a
custom-made stand to the living room floor. It was
Plexiglas outfitted with a small refrigeration unit in the
base. As Pete bustled through these excited preliminar-
ies, Estée reclined on the couch reading the *Times. Keep
an eye on personal finances this month.* Pete lit candles
and brought out a bottle of wine. Take-out Indian arrived.
They ate it off the crate.

He adopted his proud-father look, presiding over the
meal in kingly fashion. He fed samosas into his maw
with relish, smeared chutney on garlic nan, and orated.
Paging through *People*, he said, 'She got that stuff
injected in her lips, collagen or whatever. Makes them
puff out. Would you look at that pink shirt? I'm sorry, but
that man is a faggot.'

She drank glass after glass, until Pete opened a second
bottle. She was pleasantly buoyant. A homey glow
infused the carved ebony lingam, the frog mask from
Bali, and the spear-holding demon with brotherly
warmth. 'Nothing is as hard,' she mused, 'as it looks.'

'Hell yeah,' said Pete Magnus. In the dim light the sun-
lamp-tanned orb of his face shone as if polished: he was
a gleaming cherub, a round and sated doll. 'In veeno
very tass, right?'

'Not exactly *veritas*,' she said, but he stood and swept
the white boxes of food off the crate with a flourish. He
hefted a hammer and pried two nails from either side
of the crate, dropped the hammer on the couch, and
lifted the lid. Estée, still seated on the rug, peered over

the edge and saw only white Styrofoam peanuts.

'And now,' said Pete Magnus, 'for our feature presentation. Straight from Papua New Guinea.'

He dug slowly into the peanuts until he'd cleared enough away to grab both sides of a smaller box, which he extracted. He set it on top of the peanuts and opened it, pulling out a wad of waxy tissue paper the size of a softball. This he held gently on the palm of one hand as he tiptoed to the display platform, where he placed it.

'C'mere,' he whispered, and beckoned to Estée. She went to stand beside him. 'For your viewing pleasure, exclusive contraband from one of the last man-eating tribes known to the modern world,' he announced, and carefully peeled off the paper.

It took her a minute to get it. The object was slightly larger than an avocado, wrinkled like a prune and almost as dark, a mahogany tinge to it. She leaned closer: on the top she could make out strands of coarse black thread peppered with a little gray. It was riddled with craters, indentations, and bulges. A faint, sweet odor when she inhaled. The upper half shriveled, marked with two small crumbling dabs of red paint near the front, seemingly ancient. On either side, crusty flaps.

Pete Magnus stood back and she moved around to look at it straight on. Two puckered slits in front: eyes. The crusty flaps therefore ears, the threads hairs. A shrunken head. In the center of the face, a caved-in blister, no doubt referred to in happier times as a nose. It had been divested of its cranium, of teeth, bones, apparently of cartilage too; nothing remained to it but some distant descendant of skin.

'Wanted one of these things forever, you have no idea how impossible it is to get one,' said Pete Magnus. 'Is it awesome! Jesus.'

'Maybe it's not real?' she offered.

'Not real, are you kidding?' snapped Pete Magnus. 'What I paid for this, it better fuckin be real. This guy I talked to deals with the Indonesian government, coupla guys in customs there you got a few bribes, deal with the copper-ore trucks coming through from Papua, drivers have contact with people, I could tell you some stories. Problems I had. Started looking four years ago, that's how long. Persistence, Esty. *Dee*-termination.'

'I'd like some more wine,' said Estée, and headed back to the couch. Pete Magnus fiddled with the stand, closed the glass case, and bolted it at the back. He turned a dial beneath the cooling unit till it hummed.

'See you can't take shit from these guys, you set your price you keep callin, keep with it and it's gonna take awhile then *bingo!* you're home free. There's museums that would cut off their dicks for this thing, pardon my French, Esty, but it's true. They'd kill for one of these little heads. Can't blame them, it's an actual human head! This is the head of an actual person. Gives ya chills, huh?'

'An actual person,' she repeated, nodding as she swallowed, tracing a listless finger along the label Appellation Bordeaux Contrôlée. Behind her shoulder the wizened head was making its mutilated presence felt. It was blind, it was dead, but it was staring.

'I own it! I own it!' burst out Pete Magnus, and strutted crowing and preening into the kitchen, whence he bore

another bottle of wine. He uncorked it saying, 'Toast to
the head, gotta get a name for it Esty. People come over,
freak 'em out. Introduce it, go, This is my grandfather,
Peter Magnus the First! Or like, This is the head of
George Washington. Be hilarious.' He poured the wine.

'Very funny,' she concurred.

To the head,' said Pete Magnus, and drank.

Lounging on the sofa, they gazed at the TV screen.
Soldiers shot farmers with rifles as they ran from their
burning straw huts. Pete channel-surfed. Rwanda, MTV.
Correct male pattern baldness. The bottle was half
empty; she went to her room and put on her pyjamas.
When she got back to the living room, Pete had removed
his shirt.

'I'm tense, could you rub my neck Esty?'

He laid his head in her lap while she massaged his
shoulders. It was unstrenuous. Objects were not separate, every piece was contiguous, and the wine had made
her teeth grainy. These grainy teeth, connected to her
spine and to the bony digits of her fingers, connected
thereby also to the fatty sinews of Pete Magnus flesh. His
carpet led seamlessly into the wall, chairs coalesced, her
sock feet resting on the coffee table blended into a
coaster and crumpled napkin. Thatched roofs caved in,
men tumbled under rifle fire. A greeting card from elsewhere, but in code, like everything. There were no
borders between the false time of the television and the
time in the living room. The screen touched the air and
its emissions entered her lungs and her brain through
her retina. Particles from the shrunken head, invisible to
the naked eye, spun like dust motes in the space she

occupied. They drifted onto the 2-D bodies of slain tribal children, thin arms splayed on jungle foliage. Time used itself up, spun itself out.

The lips of Pete attached themselves to the crook of her arm, where a vein sprang to prominence. He applied suction, a drooling vacuum. She tried to ignore it: something unnamed was holding her attention. An old man, held in cradling arms like a baby. She had seen it somewhere. Hoisting himself up from her lap, gaining leverage, Pete Magnus osmosed into her shoulders and neck, his head bent. His mouth scoured the surfaces. He investigated new terrain with the sole sensory organ of his face, the mouth that ate, tactile and instinctive. His ancestors had foraged for kill on the plains before their cellular phones were installed, but he would deny it to the hilt. History was too bad. He could have stayed carefree, foraging for termites with long blades of grass, picking fleas from his brothers, and then, as the sun set over Tanzania, retiring to his leafy nest to sleep.

It was ludicrous, but she relaxed and sank into inertia. Pete Magnus burrowed past her garments, hair falling over his eyes. She couldn't reach her wine glass, but no sooner regretted this than abandoned the effort. He was muttering something, the words were dispensable. Intent on his labor, he wasn't looking at her face. This was a relief; the details of his features in sweating urgency were ugly like an insult. Instead she encountered his hair, a blurry silver sheen that smelled of Pert.

Over the crest of the hair, an indistinct foreground, the shrunken head stood out in vibrant sharp outlines against the wall. She focused on the head and then unfocused,

and could discern separate strands in the Magnus coif-
fure. She was increasingly sick to her stomach, and Pete
Magnus's activity, the strain and impact, weighed heavy.
'You're so hot, I always wanted to do it since I met you,'
breathed Pete Magnus. 'Don't worry, it won't hurt.'

'It's not good,' she whispered, absent. Her teeth were
soft against her tongue.

'You got your period, am I right? Put a rubber on anyway. Got one right here. Come prepared, like a Boy
Scout, wait a second, sometimes you put these things
on, it goes down. There.' She had seen the Trojans, the
Stimula Vibra Ribbed and LifeStyles, in the drugstore,
beside spermicidal jelly and Today sponges in boxes decorated with pink blooming flowers. If only Betty had
known! She, Estée, would have been contracepted. Betty
might be walking even now, walking, running, dancing
through fields of flowering pink Today sponges, her legs
mobile and lithe, her arms strong. He fumbled with it,
rolled it down over the familiar protrusion, and was
back, panting. She felt disoriented, sick, and closed her
eyes to quell the dizziness.

'My turn,' said Larry the bodybuilder, his thick fist
churning next to her face. She pulled away and was
crawling, Pete Magnus behind her on all fours with lipstick in the shape of a face on his stomach. 'My turn,'
said Larry, beating on her neck as she tried to escape
across the carpet.

'No,' she whispered, kicking at him and losing bal-
ance, scraping her chin on the floor. She saw the window
up ahead, but Larry was fast, fast and heavy. His polished
biceps clutched her around the stomach. 'It's not my

fault, go away, she squeaked, but he was riding her back.
She was a beast of burden. Her knees burned as she
dragged them both to the window, put her hands up on
the sill, and looked out. Instead of the lights of
Hollywood she was met by the old man's grinning face.
Specimen 7 breathed tapioca and chocolate into her nostrils and pushed his hoary gray tongue down her throat.
She fell back into the room, where Larry's bulk melted
beneath her back and the old man, his blue hospital robe
gaping open, was astride her from the front.

'Don't, you thief,' she said as he mauled her chest. 'Get
off!' Applause from the cheap seats: Larry was clapping
on the other side of the room. The old man tried to pry
her legs apart with liver-spotted hands, but she slipped
out of his grasp. He ran around in circles cackling, a toy
winding down, and then tottered back to the window and
climbed out. She lay gasping for relief, but the room was
still populated; on the sidelines swam blurred faces. In
surged Jesus freaks, swooping down on her with rod and
staff. They pinned her arms back. 'Ugly b-b-bug,' said
Ron. Behind them mothmen battled with guns, and
guinea pig soldiers played patty-cake in their bunkers.
She was legless, bedridden, cocooned. The Jesus freaks
were pushed off her, protesting as they went, but she
hummed 'Ave Maria' in her head to ward them off, falling
back on old custom, and the crowds dissipated.

Instead of Pete Magnus it was the head. Water rushed
in her ears, the ocean sound of a shell. 'You are a seed
pod,' said the head, and grinned toothless, its mouth
spreading and splitting. 'Betty, a man needs a son.' The
head and the demon with his spear and tufted anklets

were on her, they were fathers and sons and dead ghosts and they had her now. She remembered Helen and was gripped with panic, cold, a ball of hard ice in her stomach.

'Yes! Yes!' said Pete Magnus, but she pushed him off. 'What, Esty, what the hell?' he whinnied, his organ dangling in the air in a yellow tube sock.

She struggled to her feet, holding her stomach, and ran naked into the bathroom, where she shut herself in, breathing fast and hard. She ran water in the tub and swallowed aspirin. When she settled down in the hot water a flower of blood blossomed, crimson against the white porcelain beneath her, and faded. She had guarded against it, but then forgotten. Now it was set in stone. Somewhere someone was laughing.

Pete Magnus had invited them in. He had made an expatriate of the shrunken head, shipped it over forests and oceans. He had adopted it for his private zoo, but it did not wish to be kept. They were locked in together. It would hurt her more than it hurt him. Such was the law of fathers.

three

'They have a police record of the fire,' Pete Magnus told her, 'but there's no bones. No bones and no teeth.'

He had been contacted by Bill's attorney, who told him no one knew where Bill and Betty were. Apparently, however, Bill had empowered the lawyer to set up a fund. 'It's a trust fund,' reported Pete Magnus. 'The thing is Esty, what your crazy father did was, he made me your guardian.'

'What does that mean?' she asked. Sitting across from the shrunken head, whose crumpled eye sockets held her mesmerized, she was motionless. She had taken two Valiums from the medicine cabinet to distract from her stomach pains. She knew the source of the pains; ibuprofen, aspirin, Tylenol were no defense against them.

'This trustee, he disburses funds to me and I funnel 'em down to you,' said Pete Magnus. 'I don't know why he did it. Maybe it's how young you are'

'So if I need money,' she said, 'I have to get it from you?'

He was lounging on the couch, legs up on the coffee table, suit jacket thrown over the back of a chair. He had loosened his tie and unbuttoned his shirt, calling for a cold one as he came through the door. He took a swig and shot her a sidelong look. 'In the legal sense I guess that's the deal,' said Pete. 'But you know me, I won't be hard to handle. You wanted Esty, you could have me in the palm of your hand.'

She was queasy. She went to the bathroom and threw up in the toilet bowl.

'I should get a job,' she said when she returned. He was watching basketball.

'Problem is, with that is,' said Pete, 'you don't have a high school diploma. Plus you got no work experience, not even waiting tables. Plus you're under the weather. Don't worry babe. You're set. It's a generous allowance. You stick with me. Slam dunk!'

She was momentarily stunned, but the arrangement matched Bill's profile. She knew what she had to do. She was alone in her knowledge of the future and therefore the sole responsible party. When the time came she had to have the facts at her fingertips. Pete Magnus's doctor had diagnosed her with an ulcer, but he was wrong. She had no faith in medical professionals. They were machinists in a country of animals. The pangs they ascribed to an ulcer were in fact clear indications that the embryonic monster was attempting a jailbreak. It was trying to eat its way out, gnawing and scratching. Its dead godfather had proved unforthcoming. Frequently she asked him what she had done to deserve it, but his vocal cords had been severed long since and he refused to sing. He was unrepentant. Anyway, she blamed the middleman.

She learned about New Caledonia, about headhunters in South Massim, about the warriors of nineteenth-century Melanesia who believed that the meat of their enemies contained the vitality of the deceased – a vitality that, if ingested, was transferred through gastric juices and bloodstream to its new host, the conquering hero. Heroes who ate the vanquished, by dint of their consumption, safeguarded themselves against their victims' posthumous vengeance. Thigh meat, breast meat, arms or flanks, white or dark it made no difference.

It was not only the Papua New Guineans. There were others: domestic subspecies. She conducted hagiographical research, but on a pantheon of criminals instead of saints. Their accomplishments were a matter of public record. Daniel Rakowitz had made Manhattan dancers into soup, Arthur Shawcross had eaten eleven women after their demise, and Jeffrey Dahmer pickled genitalia and painted skulls. Then there was Chikatilo, a gourmand of tongues and private parts who liked his food still breathing. They appeared in sufficient numbers to convince her that geography was not the key. Man-eating was pandemic.

When her homunculus was born, if she survived, she would have to raise it. On the sly, with money raised by pilfering from Pete's petty cash, she enrolled in a week-long seminar she saw advertised in *Family Circle*, on a rack beside the cash register in a grocery store. Titled 'Prenatal Lessons in Happy Child Rearing,' it was hosted by an antediluvian Junior League chapter in association with Mothers Against Drunk Driving and held in a conference room at a Sheraton.

The other attendees were bulging with expectancy, distended bellies sheathed in floral cottons. Between pro forma lectures they mingled over a buffet lunch, included in the price of admission, and shared confidences on the subject of morning sickness and discharge. A woman named Pammie said she and her husband, Ray, an urban planner, were going to have at least five children. 'My sister's into Zero Population Growth, but it's mostly for welfare mothers on crack and that,' she revealed. 'I figure Ray and I would be great parents, so we should go the whole hog. There're no bad kids, just bad parents. Maybe there should be a test or something, like a minimum annual income for people who want to have kids, or like an IQ test, and you fail the test they should give you one of those Norplants or like a vasectomy,' and she scooped up a helping of ambrosia salad and trundled back to her chair.

'I don't believe that,' confided a freckled eight-monther to Estée. 'There's plenty of room. I saw on TV how they could melt the polar ice caps on Mars with nuclear bombs and then it would be warm enough to live on.'

In the afternoon, small-group discussions were held. Novice mothers sat around tables and deferred to a presiding moderator. They were required to write down child care dilemmas on scraps of paper, anonymously, and hand them up to her. She read out the questions one at a time. In Estée's group, the first question was an obvious plant. 'Your child and the president of the United States are trapped in a burning building. Which one do you save?'

'Wouldn't the Secret Service get the president out?' asked Pammie.

'That's right,' said the moderator fondly, 'your child should always be your first concern.' There followed conversations about breast pumps, sudden infant death syndrome, and potty training. 'My, we have a comedian with us today!' said the moderator, and read out Estée's question. 'Your baby is eating people. What do you do?' This was greeted with a round of titters. Estée excused herself. Evidently the professional mothers were unwilling to help.

In the library she found no reference to cannibal embryos, although some toddlers in far-off tribes were routinely trained to run with their spears. Advice on care and grooming was not forthcoming. She would have to approach Pete Magnus with the problem. After all, he was her guardian and might have to be solicited to release monies for the cause of upbringing. Over take-out Mexican, he grumbled about business problems. 'Goddamn midwestern housewives waving bills in my face, threatening litigation, do I need this Esty? Senile fathers drooling on their pillowcases and their menopausal daughters come screaming at me, old guys probably don't give a shit, practically corpses, hooked up to life support, persistent vegetative state, you can bet your ass they don't even know their own names anymore, what do they care if their windows look out on panoramas of the Sonora Mountains? Could be some back alley in Jersey City for all they care, they don't know the difference. Plane trip's gonna kill 'em?'

'I'm going to have a baby,' said Estée.

He choked on a chip doused in chunky-style salsa.

'That's impossible Esty, the doctor would've told me.

Plus which we, I mean that one time – you been going out on your own?'

'I don't know anyone but you.'

'Then you're not pregnant,' said Pete Magnus, wiping his eyes with a Taco Bell napkin. 'I know it for a fact. Just because you're late, it doesn't mean you got a bun in the oven. Jesus Esty, scared me half to death.'

'It's not a normal baby,' she said. 'It's trying to eat its way out. That's why I have the stomach pains. The shrunken head is the father. You're like Joseph.'

Pete Magnus stared at her and then folded his napkin into a small square.

'Esty,' he said with unaccustomed gentleness, 'the stomach pains are from your ulcer. We gotta get you some help. You ever been to a therapist?'

'If I have a baby, will you help me with it? That's all I want to know. That's the only reason I told you.'

'Listen Esty,' he said, leaning forward and circling her wrist with thick fingers, 'I'm here for you. But drop the baby shit. It's a fantasy. Maybe you didn't have sex ed. For babies you need your balls, Esty. Testes. You need your spermatozoa. That shrunken head has no sperms Esty. That shrunken head couldn't fuck its way out of a paper bag.'

'I read in a magazine at the doctor's that the males of a species are the ones that pass down the most bad genes,' said Estée. 'It also said: The male typically makes a swift post-coital exit, leaving the female to rear her offspring alone. And anyway the head used your sperms to do it. You have testes. I saw them.'

'Listen Esty, I'm not going to sit here teaching you the

facts of life,' said Pete Magnus. 'Let's just drop the
subject. You're not having a baby, okay?'

'You have no idea,' said Estée stiffly, and stalked into
her bedroom. She locked her door, found a discarded
lighter in a desk drawer, and burned the notebook, long
hidden in a drawer. Pete Magnus rapped on the door
when the smoke alarm went off and poured Evian on
the blaze.

Next morning, with the ersatz Joseph off to work, she
held a vigil in front of the head. She imagined the end of
his life. He had lain dying in the black soil, beneath
foliage so thick he gazed upward to the sky, flat on his
back, and saw only a glimmer from the pale nut of the
sun. Sliced open from throat to crotch, heart still flutter-
ing, viscera spilled over an anthill, he had abandoned his
carcass. He had joined the numberless ranks of the forgotten. He was inconsolable. His bones were restless; he
was at a loss in the land of opportunity. The purple
mountain majesties were not for him, nor yet the amber
waves of grain. He had been trained in the customs of his
forebears. Nothing had equipped him for a realtor. She
pitied him, no matter what he had done.

'I was talking to this woman Leola, at the office,' said
Pete Magnus from his car phone. 'She goes, what Esty
needs are female friends, like other women she can relate
to. Sisterhood and shit. So I asked this woman Marsha,
more your age. She goes yeah, she's into it. Fuck you!
Asshole tailgater, I should brake and collect his insurance, send his premiums sky-high. Lunch at a Thai
place. Take the corporate AmEx. Just you two girls. I figure it's cheaper than an analyst. You should go Esty.

Gotta get out more. Don't eat a spicy dish. With that ulcer and all.'

'She's the one that does the primal scream?'

'That's the one. But she's really a nice chick. You'll like 'er.'

Pete picked her up in the Mercedes, with Marsha in tow, and dropped them off at the restaurant. Marsha ordered satay with peanut sauce and coconut milk soup.

'It's a learning growth process,' she said, dipping her chicken. 'When I can actually express the primordial anguish, you know in this venting scream, then it's like a purging. A catharsis. I graduate and I can train other students. The course takes two years. I have another three months before the scream.'

'You can't just go ahead and scream?' asked Estée, staring as skewered chicken made vanguard assaults on the rectal ○ of glossy lips. She had no appetite for birds, reminded by their white meat of gizzards and spoor-encrusted claws.

'That would be premature,' said Marsha. 'A premature scream can traumatize you. It would set me back a year. I mean if just anyone could walk off the street and scream they wouldn't have to charge so much for courses. Like I said, it's a formative growing experience. Right now I just chant. I also sing karaoke. That's where I met my husband.' She extracted a tube of lipstick marked Koral Kreme from her purse and applied it. 'I'm so compulsive about makeup, but I mean you have to look your best. Sex equals money equals power. Lew, that's my husband, he totally hates how I wear it to bed.'

'Do you have children?' asked Estée.

'Are you kidding? I have a career. I went on the Pill when I was sixteen. Have some chicken, here. It's delicious. Not exactly lo-cal, but what the hell.'

'No thank you, said Estée. 'l don't eat much meat. My father was a butcher.'

'Are you kidding? Honey, how old are you?'

'Eighteen.'

'Jesus, eighteen? The guy's a cradle robber. You don't have, I mean, you're living with Pete, right? Listen, seriously. Has he tried anything?'

'He tried to impregnate me,' she admitted. 'I think it worked.'

Marsha dropped a satay stick in her lap.

'Damn, this stuff stains,' she said, red in the face as she dabbed at the brown mark with a napkin. 'Listen, you should stay away from Pete, I mean he comes on to everyone. He came on to *me* until he started playing softball with Lew, that's my husband, and he's been having sex with a woman at the office, Leola, and he screws around on her. And she's married.'

'Don't worry, I know all about it,' said Estée, spooning up soup. 'The biological imperative of *Homo sapiens* male is to inseminate as many females as possible. The male moves from one to another as quickly as he can, for maximum propagation. But the female of the species tries to find a secure nest, a good habitat for bringing up the young. It's biology. Reproduction of the fittest.'

'What are you, a science major?' asked Marsha, flustered. 'Listen,' she urged, 'don't tell Pete what I said, okay? I mean I work for the guy. He goes, this girl is staying at my place, friend of the family, she doesn't have friends in L.A., and I mean I'm very outgoing, I like people so I go sure. I'm just worried about you, it's a dog-eat-dog world. But don't tell him what I said, okay?'

'I don't tell him anything,' said Estée. 'He has certain functions but little comprehension.'

'Yeah right,' said Marsha. 'Tell me about it. Waiter? That Thai beer, do you have it in a lite version? Like Thai beer Lite?' and she lit up a cigarette. 'I mean he doesn't understand my therapy. He's always bugging me about it. Lew's the same way, it's a thing with guys, they're so narrow-minded. I go, Lew, I got an inner child that has to get out. This is a learning growth experience. He goes, learn and grow somewhere else. In my house I want someone who acts normal. Then he goes to a ball game and comes home blind drunk with no voice from yelling insults at the umps.'

'What's the umps?'

'Stop it, I'm serious, I'm all trying to deal with child-hood trauma, my father used to spank me and make inappropriate remarks, I only remembered it in therapy.'

'My father used to make me eat moths and conduct experiments on lower mammals,' said Estée. 'Then he put me in a cage and killed an old woman in front of me. I haven't mentioned it to anyone.'

Marsha gazed at her, spoon raised, with soup dripping off it. Then she put the spoon down with a clang against her bowl and looked at her watch.

'You know what, I just remembered I got an appoint-ment with a new client that's listing with me,' she said rapidly. 'You got Pete's credit card, right? He's deducting it. I'm really late. I'm glad we had this talk. I really have

to go,' and before Estée could say good-bye she was out
the door, purse swinging at her hip, catching a heel on
the threshold as she went out.

Estée watched her make her way down the sidewalk in
jiggling strides on her high heels, the loose one causing
her to wobble. Coming to a stop at a pedestrian crossing,
waiting for the light to change, she looked at her watch,
reapplied her lipstick, and vanished. Estée paid the bill,
left the restaurant, and studied the site of Marsha's dis-
appearance on her way to the bus stop. All that remained
was a heel.

In Pete Magnus's mailbox she found a note without an
envelope.

PRopHETEeR, wARMonger & BLAsFemuR, BuRn in HELL wiTH ALL youR monEy. LETTing Old pEopLE diE wiLL dAMn you FoREvER.

She tried to show it to him, but he was on the telephone, with his arm in a sling. 'This old sow comes up
to me, corners me in the lobby, she's all, are you an anti-
Semite? She goes, because you're shutting Holy Blossom
down, would you shut it down if it was Our Immaculate
Virgin Residence? She shoves a picture in my face, it's
like one of those mass graves full of Holocaust victims.
She goes, you think just because we're poor Hassids you
can do this to us? You think we're Hassidic so you can
herd our fathers around like they're cattle? This is what
people like you have done to the world! She goes, I
could go to the ACLU or the Anti Defamation League.

She goes, we'll sue your ass off for discrimination. Esty, did you use up the Valium? Jesus Esty, you snorting it or something?'

She left the note on the coffee table and went into the kitchen, where she found the sink overflowing, refuse clogging the drain as the tap ran. She turned it off.

'Her breath smelled like gefilte fish. I'm all, lady, I would terminate the lease on that place if it was home to Saint Goddamn Francis of Assisi preaching to the birds, if it was Ronald fucking Reagan on life support there I would terminate the lease! And she's all, you Nazi! And what does she do? I swear to God, she pushed me through the revolving door, I fall down the stairs outside there and bust my arm. Didn't even have time to get her name so I could sue her before she took off and the ambulance came. Anti-Semitic my big butt. I mean my mother's maiden name was Schwarz, you know what I'm saying? My great-uncle was a rabbi. I had a bar mitzvah, all that shit, I gave it up because they made me wear the little hat. I mean the guys braid their sideburns, you know? I go, fuck the yarmulke Mom, I'm outta here. The woman still doesn't talk to me. Yeah. Gimme the stats on Friday.' She picked up a dishrag and wiped a line of salt off the kitchen table, and the piece of curled paper beside it.

Spying from the kitchen door, she saw him put down the cordless, adjust himself to the left of his zipper with the unmaimed arm, pop the tab on his Diet Coke, and redial. He waited with his antenna pointing straight up, impassive, transparent in means but opaque in purpose. It was clear that he operated predictably, one sequence presaging the next, but why? She felt a cramp in her stomach: the baby chewing. In a wash of warm impatience she strode up behind him, grabbed the phone as he said, 'Steve?' and lobbed it across the room. It hit a Fon statue with a resounding clang and fell.

'What the fuck Esty? I just got back from the emergency room, I'm in pain here, I was attacked, I got stitches and a broken bone here, I'm in crisis and you're throwing a hissy fit? Do I get sympathy, concern? What is this?' He craned his neck and looked over his shoulder at her.

'Marsha has an inner child that's trying to get out and I've got one too.'

'I told you already, you're seeing the shrink. Now get the phone back, would you? I'm a gimp, I'm an invalid here. That was my stockbroker, he's gonna leave the office soon. Would you get me the phone? You want me to go broke?'

'Like that.' She snapped her fingers. 'Disappeared. I could too.'

'I know already. She went away and you got a Masai warrior trapped in your cervix. Okay fine. Now would you get me the phone?'

'You don't like having a broken arm, right?'

'Damn fucking straight. Now gimme the phone!'

'But an arm, it's external, it's an appendage, it's important but not necessary. Whereas a stomach or say a uterus, it's internal, it's what you are. You can't do without it.'

'Get to the point Esty, Steve's waiting here'

'You have a broken arm, I have a cannibal. If you're so upset about an arm, how would you feel about a cannibal?'

He closed his eyes and lay back, scratching at his cast with curled fingers.

'Look at it this way Esty. The cannibal's just in your head, where the broken bone is an actual fact. Now would you get the receiver?'

'You have a broken arm,' she said. 'Not a broken leg. And please stop leaving those piles of salt everywhere. I'm the one who has to clean them up.'

She turned her back on him and was heading for her bedroom when he pounced, approaching from behind as silent as a cat. Gritting his teeth, yowling from the pain afforded by his arm as it got crushed between them, he brought her to the floor. The demon warrior toppled off its end table. When she kicked Pete Magnus in the knee, he grabbed its broken spear.

'You want me to get rid of it?' he hissed. 'I'll do it right here, and then you can shut up about it.'

But he was not her primary concern. The baby had won its first victory: there was egress. She felt the rupture inside, the split sack of a balloon. The walls of the balloon were thin and punctured easily. Pete Magnus's face turned black like burnt marshmallow and he went away, along with everything.

She recognized familiar terrain by the smell before she saw it: lemon-scent disinfectant, Lysol from the golden bottle. A different room, this time private. On her bedside table plumed a vast spray of roses, in virulent orange. A thin tube fed into her arm, right inside the skin. She sighed when she knew where she was, and sighed again at the dull matte gray of the television screen bent down toward her from the ceiling. She had sighed more times than was healthy when Pete Magnus made his appearance, before any other sign of life intruded. He wore an olive suit and dark-blue tie.

'Esty, honey,' he said, placing a warm fat hand on her limp wrist. 'I need you to forgive me. You're gonna be fine.'

'Did I have a coma?' she whispered.

'No honey, no coma. You almost had a miscarriage, you had what they call one of those hemorrhages. But the baby's okay, it survived. You're fine too Esty.'

She was vindicated. She had not followed in Bill's footsteps.

'You tried to stick me with the spear.'

Pete Magnus took his hand off her wrist, clasped it in his lap, and bent his head. His cast was gone. 'I'm in counseling Esty,' he said. 'Believe me, I'm working through my hostility. My aggression was an act of self-hatred due to the fact I don't love myself enough. You don't know how rough it's been on me.'

She averted her eyes from his puffy face, more darkly tanned than she remembered. On the wall behind him hung a banner of ligatured computer printouts whose large-dot matrix letters formed the exhortation Get Well Estee.

'You had an operation,' said Pete Magnus. 'This new laser surgery. Don't worry, major medical covered it. All you got is a little scar.'

'You tried to stick me with a spear,' she repeated. The roses had no scent; from one stem a tag stuck out – 100% Silk.

'Listen Esty, when you get out we can go to counseling

together. Blame is not the point Esty. Healing is what's important. Plus you're gonna be fine.'

She gazed up at the ceiling till someone prodded her in the abdomen. It hurt. A doctor had done it. A group of young men in white coats, and two women, stood at the foot of her bed. They stared at her. They were a wall of licensed professionals. The wall was white, the wall was tall. One leaned over her from beside the mattress with a gleaming instrument. He stripped the sheet back and opened her robe.

'Interns,' said Pete Magnus.

She would not permit it. NO ENTRY signs should be posted on her front and back, all over her so that everyone saw them. They were all invasive. They put their hands and faces everywhere. They were prospectors and she was public land. 'Please go away,' she said to them. 'Don't touch me. It's inside. There's nothing you can do.'

'Esty, they're doctors. Here to help. Stay calm.'

'I don't care. Get them out!'

'Esty, don't get hysterical on me.' He moved off, took the prodding man aside, and spoke to him softly. She closed her eyes and waited. Feet shuffled. Someone blew their nose.

'Are they gone?' she asked.

'They're gone. Hey now, you can come home soon, Esty, awright?' cajoled Pete Magnus. 'Don't get yourself excited.'

'Spears,' she muttered, pensive. 'Stethoscopes.'

'Jesus, Esty, you gotta let it go. Blame is not productive. Don't forget, but forgive. Healing Esty. Healing.'

'How about Marsha?'

'Marsha?' Pete Magnus's pager was beeping. He turned
it off. 'Fuckin Marsha never came back to the office, you
musta put a bee in her bonnet Esty. Husband's clueless,
guy came in looking for her, accusing me of all kinds of
shit, I'm like, dude, hands off. I figure she dumped him
and took off. I could see why. That guy has a lot of
aggression. It's rooted in insecurity. So she split. Load off
my mind, with that chanting and shit. I was getting sick
of it. She's probably living in a commune where they
chant oogala boogala. Good riddance.'

If he refused to listen she would not waste her breath.
It was true he was stupid. He was eyeless and armless,
butting his stubby head against walls. She would take a
firm hand with him from now on. She would bide her
time, then dart out from under the rock.

'The baby deal Esty,' he said, seating himself on the
edge of the bed. 'I mean are you sure, you know, I'm the
father? No offense. But it's so weird.'

'You're responsible,' she told him. 'You bought the
head. You put him in the box. Plus you supplied the
sperms.'

'That's all I'm asking,' said Pete Magnus. 'I been
thinking, we should go away. I got some plans, an enterprise. Talk about it when you're better. Here, you know,
I got these idiots trying to sue me for terminating a
lease, making my life a living hell. They got no legal
basis, that doesn't mean they go away. I filed for a
restraining order, but that shit takes time. You ever been
to Florida?'

When visiting hours were over a doctor entered her
room. He was old: his pink face was mottled and his

earlobes hung long and flabby on each side of his head like handles on a Grecian urn.

'For your chart here, I need some information. Family medical records. Is there a history of cancer? Heart disease?'

'You name it,' she said, disinterested. 'Obesity, mental illness, chronic paraplegia.'

'Paraplegia is not a disease,' he chided, head waggling. 'I'm mainly interested in heart disease and retardation. Was there a history of that?'

'Unca Dicky had a low sperm count,' she mused. On the silken roses beside her head there crawled a silken caterpillar, spotted and hoary. 'My mother went bald and had to defecate in her bed. My father was fat and he was also crazy. Other than that I don't know. Why do you ask?'

'Hereditary conditions, we need to be informed. As your comprehensive health care providers. The fetus lived through your accident, but we have some questions about it. For instance, it has an anomalous heartbeat. Frankly, we're concerned.'

'Anomalous?'

'The heartbeat of the fetus is stable, but fast. Much too fast. We don't understand. The fetus's brain is about one-third the volume that it should be. Like the brain of a chimpanzee fetus. We're going to run some more tests.'

'Oh that,' she said, relieved.

'I'm afraid, Miss' – he consulted his clipboard – 'Kraft, that though the baby may have defects, it's too late to terminate your pregnancy. I'm sorry, but you need to know the situation. Realistically. We feel the infant may be challenged. Both physically and mentally.'

'I already know,' she said.

'I don't think you appreciate the ramifications. You're a very young single mother and in the event the baby does live beyond its first hours, you may have to bring up a difficult child. Your guardian has informed us you have access to a sizable trust fund. In that you're very fortunate.'

'You're a scientist, right? You're aware that freaks of nature do occur?'

'We don't like to call them freaks,' said the doctor sternly. Weedy gray tendrils, thin as thread, grew out of his nostrils. They were reaching out like plants toward the sun, trying to take root in her. Constant vigil was required. If she was not careful she would become a petri dish of sprouting microorganisms. She was already on her way.

'Please get away from me,' she said.

'Calm down. You're going through a difficult time. You need some time to adjust, honey,' he said, and pinched her cheek as he left.

The next day he told her their tests were inconclusive. They would conduct more research, but it would have to wait. They would document the later stages of the embryo's development. Pete Magnus wheeled her out of the hospital and drove to the back of his apartment building to avoid the picketing crowds in front. People carried signs that read Let Our Parents Die in Peace. Respect Your Elders. Big Business Is Bad Business. She was displeased when Pete showed her what he had done to her room.

'It's temporary,' he said, 'since we're relocating. I figured we could start early. Stock up and take all the stuff with us.'

There was a bassinet with frilly blankets, there were hanging plastic mobiles, toy drums, boxes of Huggies, a Jolly Jumper, stuffed animals including a hippopotamus the color of moss and a yellow dog, teething rings, rattles, potties, pacifiers, fuzzy sleepers with vinyl feet attached, nipple bottles.

'I hope you're not looking forward to a normal baby,' she warned.

'Hey, the doctor told me that it's probably a retard,' admitted Pete Magnus. 'I figure, treat it like a normal kid, maybe it'll snap out of it. Right?' He pointed out his favorite mobile, which featured floating hamburgers, French fries, and milk shakes in primary colors.

'Why are you doing this?' she asked him. What's your plan?'

'Plan? Jesus Esty,' he said, leading her back out to the living room. 'I'm the father. Plus which, we're good together. You take care of the kid, I'll take care of business so you can be comfortable. Lemme tell you what we're gonna do.'

She sat down on the couch and he brought her the pain pills and a glass of water from the kitchen. The shrunken head winked from its refrigerated case.

'I put in a bid on this property in Florida. Gulf Coast. Used to be a treatment plant in the sixties, cleaned it up, it's prime waterfront, gorgeous landscape. Not huge, but big enough. Plan is, convert it into a resort. Small but select, elite clientele, golf, put in a spa, that New Age crap the rich women from Taos are into, your herbs, your crystals, full-body massages, advertise in *Connoisseur*, *Architectural Digest*, and some retired folks' magazines, got a faggot chef from Greece lined up to do the food. You could be my partner, like my right-hand man, hostess-type shit when you have time. PR. You're good looking, you got class, supply the image. Your earthly paradise we got there. Go swimming in the morning. Sound sweet or what?'

'I don't know the first thing about being a hostess. And don't partners have to put in money?'

'You're a natural hostess. Plus for the money, that's no problem. You sign a few papers, we can liquidate the capital in your trust, sign a deal where you get an income off the place when it's up and running. A percentage. Part owner, stockholder. As your guardian I can facilitate.'

'Capital? What capital?'

'See Esty, what the trust is, it's the income off a pool of money tied up in stocks. You only have access to the income, being under twenty-one, but me, as your guardian, I got the right to convert the capital with your permission, way the fund's set up. Now it's just sitting there in these boring blue-chip stocks, like having a savings account. Hardly any return on your investment. Low dividends. Waste of time Esty. Trust me.'

'How much capital?'

'Gotta look it up Esty, don't have the figures at my fingertips, but if I had to guesstimate I'd say in the general neighborhood of seven, eight mil.'

'Seven or eight million dollars?'

'I know it doesn't seem like much to start the place with, but shit, pull in another investor or two, got it lined up, we're set to go. Small place, but luxury. That's the plan.'

It was not always easy to breathe. Her throat was a thin stalk clogged with thick air. Every item in the apartment had a price tag affixed: she had not noticed it before. The tags were as big as the items. Even the shrunken head had been assigned a dollar value. The price tags cluttered up the rooms. She was hemmed in by potential transactions. Reaching for her water glass, she had to brush the sofa's tag off her knee. The glass itself was marked Tiffany, $68. When she lifted the glass from the coffee table it left a ring, and in the center of the ring, $499. She put the capsules onto her tongue. They were acrid.

'Your interest in me is purely financial,' she said when she had swallowed. 'Your stake is my money.'

'It hurts me that you say that,' said Pete Magnus, shaking his head. As he did so several price tags were dislodged and fell like paper snow onto his shoulders. 'I'm the father of your child. Take care of you, put a roof over your head. I've done it *all* for you, Esty. I'm *here* for you.'

The shrunken head smirked at this and sent his vestigial body to perform a mocking dance on the mohair rug.

'Why did he make you my guardian? He hardly even knew you. Why'd he give you control of that money?'

'What can I say?' shrugged Pete Magnus. 'I'm like the Prudential rock. And on this rock He builds His church, and shit. But seriously, he probably didn't think you'd need it before you were twenty-one. The guy thought we were getting married. Jesus, he was in a world of his own. You can't figure out a lunatic. Probably thought you'd come running home to him if you had problems. How could he know his house was gonna burn to the ground the week after?'

'You said you thought they'd sold it to developers,' she murmured. 'You said it was part of their plan. A week after? How do you know when he set up the trust?'

He stood, went to the far wall, and ransacked his antique writing desk, never used by current owner, mint condition, $3,599, for a crumpled pack of Marlboro reds. Extracting one bent cigarette, he dropped the pack and went back to scrounging. 'Just trying to make you feel better,' he said. His face belied the casual assertion. It was a swollen beet against the yellow spit of flame from his lighter. It burgeoned with nervous blood, angry capillaries pulsing under the skin.

But she was tranquil now. Her new knowledge baptised the desert of the penthouse, streamed over the items and tags, blurring the dollar signs, voiding the digits. It cleansed her of confusion. It was drowning Pete Magnus.

'When did you know about it? I mean the trust?'

'When I told you Esty, Christ.' he said, spitting a fleck of tobacco off the tip of his tongue. 'The lawyer contacted me.'

'Then how do you know when he did it? Why did you say he didn't know the house would burn? Before you said he burned it down himself. That's what you said.'

'Figure of speech Esty,' rushed Pete Magnus, taking a deep drag. A cough hurtled out.

She waited, staring at him, then cleared her throat and spoke slowly. 'I can see the forest for the trees.'

'The hell does that mean?'

'I was trained to observe animal behavior,' she said softly. 'I know how to watch. You knew about the trust, and being the executor. You didn't know if he would let you keep the money. Marsha said money is power. Then the house burned.'

'Jesus, Esty, is this gratitude?'

Silence would be her acid test. She sat without movement, the infant flailing and scratching but confined, safely enclosed, in her motionless hide with insulated walls. Squinting Magnus was watery-eyed from the smoke. He bent over, brooding, in his jungle of paper, as the curlicue of nicotine, formaldehyde, and tar dispersed above them.

'You saying you don't trust me?' he sputtered at long last. Her suspicions were grounded in unprovable fact, built on a foundation of subterranean steel, invisible yet unassailable.

She kept her counsel.

'I mean what are you asking me here?' he persevered, seating himself on the edge of the couch, tapping his ash into her empty water glass.

'I thought he was the pyromaniac,' she whispered. 'But it was you.'

Pete Magnus inhaled too swiftly and choked, wracked by spasms, as smoke billowed from his nose and trickled out his coughing mouth.

'That's insane Esty,' he gasped when he could, grinding his cigarette out distractedly. 'Tomorrow we're going to counseling.' He picked up her water glass, tipped it up to his mouth, spat out the ashes, and ran to the kitchen.

'No,' she sighed into his wake. He was a fire starter. It confirmed her worst fears. Out there, alive or dead, Bill and Betty were doing what they'd always done. They had not recanted. They had made no sacrifice and no reversal. They were what they had always been. If they were living, they were living with no regret, on parallel courses, continuing as they had planned to continue. If they were dead, they were not suicides. They were dead criminals, not saints self-martyred on their knees. They had been struck down where they stood, spears raised, eyes forward, suspecting nothing. There had never been spectacular conversion.

Pete Magnus, tail between his legs, was gargling over the kitchen sink a broken man. She saw it in his slump of apathy. When she came in he didn't raise his eyes, just turned to spit into the sink, over spaghetti-sauced stoneware and matching utensils caked with meat, bracing himself against the counter's edge. She owned something. She had leverage. Anyway, the crime was unproven, and Betty had been waiting a long time for the *pax romana*.

'I have nowhere else to go,' she said. 'I can make you a loan, interest free. It comes due when I turn twenty-one.'

He turned to face her, wiping his mouth with a paper towel.

'The full amount?'

'But it's a loan.'

'Jesus Esty,' he said. 'Shit yeah!'

She headed for her bedroom, where she picked up the

icons of the baby cult and threw them out her door into a heap in the hallway. Pete made piles of salt on the living room table and sniffed them up, and then he went out. She stayed awake, seated beside the head in the living room, gazing out the window at the pattern of lights in the dark. She saw herself in Florida, cross-legged on a checkered picnic tablecloth, a quaint wooden basket beside her, wasps and gnats circling and diving beyond her reach. The rolling green lawns of her future spread out beneath her, bright as astroturf as she sipped ice tea in the shade of a date palm, casting no shadow. A few yards away, in diapers, the cannibal baby chortled and clapped its hands, crawling and tripping until it stood upright and took its first experimental steps across the grass.

part three

canibalis horribilis

one

Little Bill, as Pete liked to call him, weighed in at fifteen pounds newborn. Anesthetized for delivery, Estée never knew how they did it. Cranes, bulldozers, pulleys. There were yellow pustules on his scalp and a full set of teeth in his mouth, and he was strong and hungry enough at three days to eat a toenail off his own foot.

Pete Magnus began by playing the dutiful father, plying his son with gifts of athletic equipment and filling the nursery with gleaming trophies of his adolescent sports prowess. Baby-blue shelves were lined with red and purple ribbons, brass-colored figurines wielding discuses and shot puts, silver cups and mounted plastic barbells. One slow summer afternoon, when Little Bill lay spent and sleeping in his crib, numb from the fervor of hyperactivity, Pete leaned over the side of the crib and whistled the tune to 'Oh, Sweet Mystery of Life at Last I've Found You,' and was gouged in the cheek with a diaper pin. On the subject of his son's giant stature and rampant growth spurt, however, he waxed proud. 'Boy's gonna be a linebacker, you wait and see,' he told Estée.

An obstetrician's lawsuit brought against them after William's angry birth – pain, suffering, and medical costs for the functional loss of a thumb joint – constituted early warning to Estée, but Pete took the ordeal in stride. His son was a strapping lad, a powerhouse, a marvel of genetic engineering. He would build empires and feast on a breakfast of champions.

First it was flies, cockroaches, slugs, and worms. During his first month, already crawling, William ingested four wasps and part of a poison berry bush when Estée's tired head was turned and had to have his stomach pumped. This operation turned up, along with organic mulch, a waxy fragment of milk carton, a two-inch bolt, and a sodden box of Playtex.

By the second month, like grandfather, like son, he had graduated to avifauna. When Estée took him outside to play, praying the cadaverous cast of his skin could benefit from ultraviolet exposure, extinction rates soared. Flycatchers and vireos made themselves scarce, leaving only the stubborn cowbirds to nest along the fringes of the golf course. Often Estée was forced to run interference for William with the elderly guests.

'We visited the Cistern Chapel,' said a woman who had stopped beside Estée's lawn chair to chat about a guided tour of Rome. Estée gazed past her blue hair to the base of a tall tree, where William squatted in his pen in a bright pool of sun, his Dodgers visor glinting. A wind-blown feather skittered over the grass and clung to one varicose nylon. 'It was pretty, but not like the Hilton. At the Hilton they gave us itty-bitty cheeses. They had the taps that go on when you stand at the sink and water fountains right beside the toilet.'

Estée walked past her to the tree. William's chin and

mouth were muddy with blood; he held a wingless sparrow in one chubby hand. Its beak opened and closed without sound. 'Bad,' she told him sternly. 'Dirty.' She knocked the bird out of his grasp, kicked it deftly to death, and knelt to clean his face with a Baby Wipe.

'Ooh,' said the old lady, coming up behind them. 'Here's a widdle baybee.'

William bared his teeth and spat out a feather.

'Ooh! Stinky baby!'

Pete Magnus threw a three-month birthday party for William complete with tooting paper horns, a cake in the shape of a palm tree, and pipe-cleaner monkeys for the cocktail straws. Female guests attended en masse for the sake of a few free mimosas, cooing over William's bulk and manual dexterity while slyly pretending not to notice his ugliness. Even on good days Little Bill looked like tenderized beef and smelled like raw sewage. 'Now, don't worry dear,' remarked a melanoma-dappled Daughter of the American Revolution. 'He's just rashy. My first was homely as a child and now he's married to Miss Teen Ohio.'

A securities trader presented Pete with a BB gun to hold in trust for Little Bill, but the birthday boy found it and fired it at a dowager's eyeball. The missile's trajectory met tinted plastic lenses and the woman went unharmed, but after the party Pete felt it was necessary to discipline his son. Estée was alerted by guttural choking noises from the nursery and ran in to find William seated on his progenitor's windpipe, jamming a stubby arm down Pete's throat up to the elbow. When Estée pulled William off, Pete was livid and gasping. 'Get me to a mirror!' he said, and raced to the bathroom door to check himself out. When he returned he had regained partial composure. 'That dangling thing?'

'The uvula,' said Estée. 'Grape, in Latin.'

'That little shit hadda holda my uvula. Thought he was giving me a goddamn tonsilectomy.'

'Naughty William,' reproved Estée. 'Daddy needs his dangling thing.'

'Take a look in my mouth Esty. Swolled up like a bladder!'

Later Pete insisted he had been faking his terror. Estée noted, however, that he avoided William for a week and was religious in his application of tan-toned cover-up to the bruises on his neck. He touched up constantly with the aid of a Q-tip and told people he had cut himself shaving. 'Kid doesn't need assertiveness training,' he joked wanly to Estée in private.

Shortly thereafter William began to crawl out of his room and make nocturnal hunting forays, leaving his bloodied kills at the foot of Pete's bed, entrails rent asunder. They ran the gamut from mice to gulls. At first Pete was brave in the face of the evidence. 'Boys will be boys,' he proclaimed staunchly the first time he awoke to find William kneeling on his chest with a rat between his teeth. 'Hey Esty, did he get a rabies shot?'

But his bravado was only for show. In increments he transferred his attentions to management, ordering Armani suits cheap from Hong Kong, circulating among the guests and kitchen staff with claps to the back and jocular remarks, driving golf carts past the pool with a cheery wave to the swimmers. When he got out of bed in the morning he carefully stepped past the remains of small prey and locked himself in the bathroom to shave, leaving Estée to clean up the mess. Little Bill persisted with his offerings until he found the straw that broke the camel's back. Pete had left his educational reading, a paperback tome entitled *Money or Your Life*, on the carpet beside his bed. While he slept the deep sleep of the guiltless, Little Bill laid a gift on top of it: a skunk with its scent glands split open.

'Fuck him,' said Pete, putting his foot down. 'I don't care if he's the fruit of my loom. He's an asshole.'

It was clear that they had a security problem. Locks and windows were no match for William, who resisted confinement. Cleaned vermin bones piled up beside his carton of toddler-size Huggies; at night he scratched holes in the wallboard, ripped the plastic covers off electrical outlets, and stuck his tongue into sockets. Estée attempted to funnel his energy into educational tasks: she bought him 3-D puzzles, xylophones, and Tonka trucks, but William swallowed the star-shaped puzzle piece, chewed on wheels, and stuck xylophone parts up a dachshund.

The nightly expeditions did not abate, so she tried locking him in at night with a bolt outside his door. This tactic met with instant failure. William refused to eat baby food, and when she force-fed him he disgorged the pabulum onto furniture and clothes. Afraid of a hunger strike, she stopped shooting the bolt. Natural selection was the name of the game and William was top of the food chain.

A decorator named Charise was invited to stay in a

guest suite free of charge while she redesigned the pool-room. Her toy poodle, Lili, whom she festooned with pink ribbons, walked past William's window at twilight. The cadences of Charise's voice grew familiar. 'Here Lili,' she sang. 'Little pretty Lili, come to pretty Mommy.' Every evening William pricked up his ears at the sound and ran to his window to sit on the ledge in silent vigil. His rapt eyes followed Lili as she trotted past, though his head did not turn. When, beneath a balmy red sky on a Tuesday, Lili escaped her rhinestone-studded leash and disappeared onto the darkened expanse of the first fair-way, Estée was drinking coffee in the clubhouse kitchen. The poodle search was launched without her knowledge and ended when Lili was discovered shivering on the second green, emitting a high-pitched whine, with only three legs remaining.

To placate Charise, Pete had Lili fitted out with a pros-thesis and paid for canine psychotherapy. 'Florida panther,' he told Charise decisively, though there were rumored to be only five left alive in the state. Estée found a pink poodle ribbon in William's crib; she kept her mouth shut but decided to take action. She set up a twelve-foot Rent-a-Fence in a forested back lot behind the groundskeeper's toolshed, and there, beneath a canopy of trees, sequestered herself with William.

With a small tent pitched beside his playpen, a cook-stove, and a Port-a-John at her disposal, she whiled away the warm days watching while he learned to climb trees. He was happiest high in the boughs, sucking his thumb, head cocked to one side, listening. He eschewed diapers and defecated in holes in the ground; he would not be hand-fed, but grabbed his bottle from her and scampered up his favorite tree with it dangling from his mouth, rubber nipple clenched between his teeth.

At first she padlocked the fence at night, leaving William to his arboreal nest, built out of refuse and leaves, and retired to her bedroom. Soon, however, she became accustomed to her tent; she distrusted the padlock, for William was agile and canny. She began to sleep outside and entered the house only for newspapers and magazines, cassettes to play for William on her portable tape recorder, freeze-dried food, water, and changes of clothes. Pete Magnus was not pleased, since she avoided the guests and neglected her hostess duties. 'Esty, what the hell are you thinkin?' he asked repeatedly. 'Nature's for hippies Esty, hippies and Indians. Let's face it, Esty. Nature sucks.'

Her showers became less and less frequent, as did her changes of clothes. William was her sole companion and he possessed no aversion to filth. The two of them developed rituals. At the break of dawn he scavenged for rodents; she watched him eat them and carry the bones and claws to his hiding places. While she spooned up cereal, perched on a stump, William loped around the fence's perimeter, scouting for changes in the terrain. She began to notice small processes: ants flowing in a single-file river from rock to rock, the decomposition of cicadas, the mating habits of flies, the growth of weeds, the displacement of dirt churned up by her feet. She learned to tell time by the position of the sun and to feel the onset of rain from humidity in the air. She waved to the gardeners when they passed the fence, observed the distant

movements of golfers, and read to William from the
newspaper. His favorite lullaby consisted of stock-market
quotes. 'Analog: trading volume 1142, high 36¼, low
35⅜, close 35½, down ¾. Anheuser-Busch: trading volume 7889, high 50⅜, low 50, close 50⅜, up ¼. Ann
Taylor: trading volume 573, high 41⅞, low 41¼, close
41¾, no change.' At night she played him an old record-
ing of the Agnus Dei, and he fell asleep with his thumb
in his mouth, curled up in his nest in a fork in the
boughs.

On a placid Saturday, after lunch, he pronounced his
first words. She was unprepared. She'd just put down
the *National Enquirer*, which she had read aloud, and
was stretching out to sunbathe. William squatted in a
pile of leaves, picking apart a daddy longlegs.

'First ladies,' he said, casting aside a leg. 'Leading
ladies. Every lady deserves a Bill Blass original.'

Stunned, she sat unmoving as he dropped the remains
of the spider and rummaged for an old bird bone, which
he picked up and gnawed.

'What William? What?'

'Eight ways you can make every evening a fun family
night,' said Little Bill. 'Ho-hum! America's most boring
hubby spends all his time hunting fire ants.'

'Say something else!' she urged. 'William! It's a miracle!'

'Dirt-poor kid from cotton farm makes millions selling
mufflers,' said Little Bill casually, and stuck the bone into
a nostril. 'The sky's the limit: granny graduates from col-
lege at age seventy-one. Doctor discovers proven psoriasis
treatment!'

She ran into the house, where she found Pete Magnus

dressing down a busboy for drinking Red Dog on the job.

'Pete,' she panted excitedly. 'You have to hear it. He's talking! He's talking!'

Sighing, Pete Magnus followed her out to the enclosure. 'That's impossible Esty,' he complained as she unlatched the gate. 'The kid's just passing wind.'

'No, Pete,' she said. 'He was talking in complete sentences! From the newspaper. He's a genius!'

William was sitting beside a stump, twiddling a finger in his belly button.

'Uh-huh,' said Pete Magnus. 'Okay. Let's hear it.'

'Come on William. Talk!'

'Buddy,' said William. 'Buddy buddy bud.'

'That's great Esty,' said Pete Magnus, consulting his watch.

'No, he was really talking before,' she said. 'William, come on. Do it again.'

William burped and cooed, wiggling his fingers.

'Look Esty, I got a meeting with the accountant,' said Pete. 'Gotta go.'

William crawled to the fence to watch him leave.

'Give news anchorman the ax,' he said solemnly. 'Four out of five in survey say.'

After the first outburst, his phrasemaking was sporadic. He spoke seldom, but eloquently. 'Stock market rebounds,' he remarked when she dropped a soup can on her foot. 'Veteran market watchers credited technical factors for much of the buying.' He placed a twig on the ground beside her while she was brushing her teeth at the garden hose and said, 'Total diabetes care. At your

Wal-Mart pharmacy department.' Bursting into the Port-a-John, he delivered a lengthy monologue. 'Pope John Paul launches Eastern European trip. Korea's Christians: a surging, prayerful force. As many as 500 million sperm start their arduous journey at the opening of the cervix.'

She tried to instigate conversations, but William refused to engage. He was a soliloquist. She kept track of his statements and read to him constantly to improve his vocabulary, whatever she found in the lobby. Systematic patterns emerged. When he was hungry, he said, 'Introducing the Infiniti I30.' When he was very hungry he switched to, 'Benson Hedges 100's: the lengths you go to for pleasure.' There were stock translations. 'Look at this dead animal' was 'Ten dollars for happy thoughts. Send your entry.' 'You can't have it, it's mine' was 'The incredible chopper, ultimate cutting machine.' He did not speak when spoken to, but he was learning fast.

Then came the ornithologists.

They were garbed in camouflage and golfing gear; they had binoculars and cameras hanging around their necks. They gathered at the fence and gawked at the foliage. Estée, with ratty hair and grimy arms, hid behind the Port-a-John and watched them. It was midafternoon. William was napping.

'It must be a campsite,' said a fat man in a tank top. 'See? A little one-man tent.'

'Right here? On the grounds? I'm surprised they allow it,' offered a woman in floral shorts.

'Lookit that,' said the first one, and pointed. 'See? Way on up there! Big old nest! Lonnie, look through your glasses. It could be endangered. Size of that thing!'

'Somethin in there,' said Lonnie. 'Can't tell what it is, though. Whaddaya think, Amy Lee?'

'There *is* something in the nest,' said Amy Lee. 'It's not moving. Maybe it's dead.'

'Throw a rock at it. It'll fly out.'

'Here we go, here we go,' said Lonnie.

'I don't know if you *should*,' objected Amy Lee. 'A rock?'

'Just a little one, Amy Lee. Barely a pebble. Ready Lon? I'll aim the telephoto. You got good aim? On the count of three. Hold on a second.'

'Stop!' said Estée, running out into view. They turned to stare at her, but the first stone was cast. It hit the trunk beneath William's nest; he raised himself on all fours, groggily, from sleep.

'My Jesus Lord, it's a baby!' A shutter clicked.

'Go away,' said Estée. 'Leave! Go!'

'But it's a naked baby,' said Amy Lee.

'Lady, he must be thirty feet up! What are you, crazy? Put your kid up a tree?'

They were distracted by the sight of William crawling out onto a limb.

'He'll fall to his death!'

'He's not going to fall,' said Estée. 'Just get out of here.'

'Jesus, Lonnie, get it on the camcorder. Tarzan boy!'

William swung down from branch to branch while the bird-watchers gaped.

'You could make a mint with that baby,' said Lonnie.

'I told you to leave!' said Estée, and ran toward them. 'Get out of here! It's private property!'

They backed off as she approached. The camcorder

followed William down his tree to the ground. He loped toward the bird-watchers, giggling. At the fence he sat on the ground and gazed at them.

I got it on tape,' said Lonnie. 'I got it!'

'Aqua-Ban eliminates monthly water bloat,' announced William. 'Christie Brinkley fights vicious gossip. Crooked socialite swindles her pals out of $69 million. Those divorce rumors are garbage!'

'Holy shit,' said Lonnie.

Half an hour after they left, Pete Magnus appeared at the fence in casual attire, without a tailored jacket.

'Esty,' he announced, 'forget this back-to-nature shit. The guests are freaked out. I hadda tell my man Daniel to steal their lousy videotape. Little Bill is going into full-time day care. I mean it Esty. And you're coming back to the house.'

'I am not,' said Estée. 'We're fine out here.'

'We agreed Esty. Nothing that would jeopardize our investment. You have to act like a regular mother. They're coming to get the fence in two hours. That's it.'

'But he has to be outside. He needs it, Pete. He doesn't like the indoors. We shouldn't force it on him.'

'Day care Esty. I found a place already. He can't live like this. It just encourages him. He's gotta learn to be like a normal kid. You know, Ninja Turtles, Barney the Dinosaur, and shit. Get 'im in front of the TV Esty, teach him what's what.'

'He's not a normal kid. You know that.'

'And he'll never get normal if you let him run around with no clothes on. I don't know how I let you do this in the first place Esty. But I can't be everywhere at once. I

got a business to run and so do you. He starts on Monday.
I told 'em he was two. He's so big they won't know the
difference. And take a shower. You gotta look good for
the guests. You're dressed like a homeless person.'

'Don't do it,' said Estée. 'Don't make him come down
from the trees.'

William crawled up and sniffed her foot and then
watched closely as Pete strolled back to the putting
green.

'Ritual slaying in sleepy Arkansas town,' he said
softly.

t w o

'We describe ourselves as a full-service day care for difficult toddlers,' they told her over the phone. 'We pride ourselves on both sensitivity and tough love. A troubled toddler has many conflicting needs. Toddling is a time of big decisions, including toy selection, formation of attachments, potty use, and even weaning.'

They agreed to steward William sight unseen. They'd fed Pete Magnus a harder line than they gave her: no spoiled boy would prove immune to their authority. Even the most stubborn infants, over time, would yield to their unwavering dogma Spare the Rod.

She would have to drive there and back every day, and Pete Magnus's truck would be unsafe. William could not be permitted to have free range within the cab. It was a confined space and high-speed collisions might occur as a result of his frantic activities. A pediatrician had once prescribed Ritalin to calm him down, but Estée knew no chemical lullaby would work on William. Instead of resorting to sedatives, she bought an old prison van at a state vehicle auction and redecorated its interior. She bolted down a small fiberglass tree, lined the floor with cedar chips, leaves, and twigs, and ordered an anthill in a sandbox for placement in the corner. She could keep an eye on William in the rearview mirror, through the mesh. Other drivers would steer clear, due to the faded, chipped print on the rear of the van. CORRECTIONAL TRANSPORT: HIGH-SEC. KEEP WELL BACK.

'Shop where your money buys more!' crowed William gleefully when he saw it, clapping the heels of his hands. It was his seal of approval.

'Jesus Esty, we'll get laughed outta town,' said Pete, surveying it in passing through his Ray-Bans.

'Factory clearance,' grumbled William when his father had turned the corner. 'Slashed prices. Total liquidation.'

Debbie Does Day Care ran a tight ship. The building was part warehouse, part bunker, set at the rear of a flat gravel lot, with small windows above eye level and an outside mural of Bambi sniffing daisies. William wore diapers on his first day, beneath a pair of brand-new Osh Kosh B'Gosh overalls, and carried a mouse skull in his zippered pocket for security. He'd never had a favorite blanket.

They were greeted by Caregiver Ann at the entrance. Her name tag featured a happy face and bore the legend Love Hurts. Inside, the walls were thick and soft, sterile marshmallow white. Estée handed over her personal check and was offered a tour of the premises. William scuttled along at her side as they were led through a maze of quiet corridors whose bulletin boards sported crayon pictures of hearts and rainbows. The recreation room was a factory space three stories high. Here, the Caregiver told Estée, was where most of a Typical Day would be spent. The floor was padded wall to wall, and the walls were padded

up to six feet off the ground. There were lined pits built
into the foam-covered concrete, like swimming pools with
no water. Along the back wall huge multicolored balls big
as boulders were lined up on a rack.

'The playpens,' said Caregiver Ann. She indicated one
of the pits, easily five feet deep with rounded edges. 'You
see how safe the toddlers are. We have a lot of naughty
little ones who like to practice self-mutilation. A
Caregiver pats them down when they enter. We do not
like a sharp object.'

'What do they do for fun?' asked Estée.

'They stay in the pits during play hours,' said the
Caregiver sternly. 'They play with body balls or Bouncy
Ponies. Beanbag rocking horses. Most toys on the com-
mercial market aren't geared toward troubled toddlers.
Excuse me. My pager.'

She went into the office. William had his eye on
another Caregiver stacking mats in the corner with her
back turned.

'Shelley Winters: acting turned me into a pill-popping
addict,' he remarked, and touched his mouse skull
through denim.

'Sorry,' said Caregiver Ann briskly, snapping closed a
portable phone as she strode out of the office. 'We have
learning hour, social expression hour with a JD counselor,
vegan lunch, nap time, and interactive psychological support games. No utensils of course. We stress cooperation
and confidence. Other questions?'

'How many children are there?' asked Estée, distracted.
William was squatting on his haunches, stuffing a blue-
bottle fly in his mouth.

'We have ten toddlers now,' she told Estée. 'We have to keep enrollment low. This is an exclusive service.'

'It's very important,' said Estée, as she was led toward the exit with William trotting beside her, 'that he doesn't get out of the building. He can be a bit destructive.' She knelt to remove a small wing from the corner of his mouth. 'Okay William. I'm leaving, but I'll be back tonight. Be good.'

She was at the van, opening the driver's-side door, when he dashed out, scrambled up her legs, and threw his arms around her neck.

'William,' she said, 'it's just during the day. You'll be fine.'

'Wild bachelor party,' he mumbled plaintively in her ear. 'With seventy-two topless dancers!'

'William, get off,' she said. 'I'll be back this afternoon. Come on. You're a big boy.'

He clambered around to her front by holding onto her head. 'You can't rush smooth flavor,' he urged.

'Down, William.'

Caregiver Ann looked on, with William grubbing disconsolately in the pebbles at her feet for stray worms, as Estée got into the van and reversed out of the parking lot.

At the resort she wandered across the grounds with nothing to do. Pete Magnus, friendly and avuncular, put an arm around her shoulders and introduced her to a guest with a colostomy bag. 'Esty, meet Don "Tiger" Tindale,' he boomed. 'A colonel, retired. He used to play golf with Dick Nixon. Go figure!'

'Got yourself a pretty little wife there,' said Don Tindale, hefting his nine iron appreciatively and nodding into the distance. 'My first wife was quite a filly too. Cunt like a vice though. Had to pry it open with a crowbar.'

'I'm sorry, what?' said Estée.

'Ha!' said Pete Magnus. 'Ha ha. That's a good one, Don.'

Estée floated with equal buoyancy in air and water; her hands were not tied. She was light as helium. She could study the sky without watching her back. In the afternoon, having left Pete Magnus in conversation with a senile poultry distributor from Milwaukee, she laid down a towel over the damp grass beside an imitation Chinese pagoda in Pete's garden of orchids and fell asleep.

Caregiver Cindy, wearing a name tag inscribed Idle Hands, let her into the rec room at 5:30. Caregivers in padded body armor, like Michelin men, stood with arms akimbo, supervising the play. Little Bill was cross-legged, a bulky Buddha in the corner of a pit. He held a Nerf football in his lap and shredded it methodically as other toddlers waddled and fell in the piles of shredded foam, righting themselves on unsteady bow legs and then falling again. One of them stood up, supported himself against the pit wall, and trundled toward William holding a panda in a drooping felt hat. He held it out to William, who dropped the fragments of the ball and grabbed the bear. The toddler bent down and retreated. William bit off a panda ear as the boy sucked on a piece of foam and cautiously, from time to time, peeked out from under downcast lids.

At 6:00 P.M. sharp the Caregivers corralled the children and made them stand in a line.

'Thank-you time,' said Caregiver Ann brightly. 'Now is when we thank the Caregivers for a fun-filled, developmental day. Douglas, you start.'

'Tank oo,' said the toddler who had proffered the panda.

'You're welcome, Douglas. Andy?'

'Dank oo,' said toddler number two.

'You're welcome, Andy. William?'

'Buddy,' said William. 'Buddy buddy bud.'

Mothers, keys jangling, heels churning up gravel as they crunched over the lot to the door, converged in the entryway.

'How was he?' Estée asked Caregiver Cindy.

'His linguistic abilities are stunted,' said the Caregiver. 'For a two-year-old, he's challenged. All he says is birdy. We think he may have had an early bird trauma.'

'Ha,' said Estée. 'Ha ha. That's a good one.'

'This place is a godsend,' stage-whispered a fat mother beside Estée. Douglas clung to her leg. 'I was getting run ragged!'

'We try to instill the social tools they'll need for kindergarten,' explained Caregiver Cindy. 'Tomorrow the children will be playing noncompetitive games, including I'm Normal, You're Normal: A Game of Discovery. It's a popular favorite.'

'Wonderful,' said Douglas's mother, and patted at the pancake makeup on her chin with a flowered Kleenex. 'Stop it, Douglas. You stop it!' He was wiping his nose on her knee. She plied the Kleenex underneath his nostrils and he settled on the ground, sucking his thumb. William was face to face with him. As the mother fumbled through her purse and pulled out a mirrored compact,

William reached out and poked Douglas on the chest. Estée watched as Douglas looked up slowly, removed his glistening thumb from his mouth, and then, with fluid grace, fell onto all fours in front of William. He scoured the floor with splayed, chubby fingers and was hastily eating dust when his mother clicked her compact shut, screeched, and swooped down to pick him up.

'Douglas! Filthy!' she chided. 'It's a relapse!' She pried open Douglas's mouth and extracted a dust bunny. Douglas's mouth hung slack, his rubbery lips manipulated by his mother as he kept his eyes trained on William. Douglas's mother flapped her hand hysterically, trying to shake loose the debris. It clung first to her thumb, then to her forefinger, then back to the thumb. 'Disgusting! Cindy, look! He hasn't done this in months!'

'Remember the three S's for productive parenting: support, straight talk, and swift punishment. It is the only way they learn,' rebuked Caregiver Cindy.

On the gravel of the parking lot, before Estée lifted William into the back of the van, she picked him up and looked into his eyes. He regarded her solemnly.

'William,' she whispered, 'they didn't hurt you, did they?'

'Famed fat man slims down by eating donuts,' said William. 'Six-hundred-pound circus freak goes on a donut diet.'

'William! What a good boy!'

She loaded him in, dried grateful tears on her shirtsleeve, and drove home singing 'Panis Angelicus,' while William leapt and swung happily on the limbs of his fiberglass tree.

The next day, with Little Bill remanded once more into Caregiver custody, she ambled from bush to bush snipping bulbous orchids off their stems and sticking them in vases, swam in the ocean, and played a halting tennis game with a one-armed ex-Marine in his sixties. Pete Magnus kept busy downing Singapore slings poolside with a tight-faced widow. In a moment of solitude, looking out her open bedroom window at a dying palm tree that reminded her of home, she thought she could hear a melody in the fronds. 'As the tree grows,' it went, singsong, 'so grows the branch.' In the pause that followed, a sea-scented breeze lifted the sheer drapes over the hardwood floor, the pregnant stomachs of long white women.

She vowed to enjoy her new leisure, but during a conversation about lo-cal cooking with a diet counselor from Santa Barbara, and later while she was floating her arms atop the surface of a bubbling Jacuzzi, she felt unease, like an itch in space, gone as soon as she turned to face it. It was the hair in a movie projector, trembling at the edge of the frame.

When she went to pick up William on his second day, Caregiver Lisa and Caregiver Cindy cornered her and delivered a sermon on bad behavior. 'Little Bill's disturbing the dynamics here,' said Caregiver Cindy.

'What do you mean?' asked Estée.

'William is a ringleader,' said Caregiver Lisa. 'He excites the other toddlers and resists discipline. During I'm Normal he forced another boy to urinate on himself.'

'What can I do?' asked Estée.

'Talk to Caregiver Ann,' said Caregiver Cindy.

Caregiver Ann solicited a check. Hazard insurance.

On the third day, Caregiver Cindy took a leave of absence. Estée saw her limp across the parking lot to her Mazda, whose personalized plates said HOTMAMA, with her right hand wrapped in gauze. Caregiver Ann informed Estée that it was William's fault, but offered no further details. When Estée went to pick him up on day four, the toddlers were hunched around him in the pit, squatting, heads bowed. William, in his usual cross-legged stance, stared straight ahead, unmoving except for his chubby fists held in his lap, fingers twitching.

'They look like they're behaving well to me,' she told Caregiver Kim.

'We were forced to inflict a group punishment,' said the Caregiver. 'Look what they did to Lisa!'

Caregiver Lisa emerged from behind a file cabinet with her frizzy blond hair in disarray, sniffling and wiping her nose. Her blue eyeliner was smeared. On closer inspection Estée noticed a large bald patch on the side of her head. One earring hung from her left ear: a bright, bobbing Minnie Mouse head. The right ear was bloody.

'William did that?' she asked.

'No,' snapped Caregiver Kim. '*They* did it *for* him.'

'That's ridiculous,' said Estée.

'Talk to Caregiver Ann,' said Caregiver Kim.

'Four grand,' said Ann. 'Pain and suffering for Lisa, and she'll sign a waiver. Plus all her medical expenses, no questions asked. Those little bastards tore her earlobe open.'

'What does it have to do with William?'

'You can either pay up,' said Caregiver Ann, 'or get him out of here right now.'

'William,' said Estée, opening the back doors of the van, 'have you been bad?'

'One kidney saves two lives,' said William, and hopped into the sandbox. 'Beat wrinkles by growing houseplants.'

'Bullshit,' opined Pete Magnus when she advised him of the situation. 'They're only little kids, how much damage can they do? Anyway, those gals are paid to take care of them. They're responsible for the brats. Can't prove a thing. They know you're a soft touch Esty. Debbie Does Daytona is ripping us off.' He sat on his bed, unloading a shipment of Ferragamo loafers wholesale from the manufacturer as William pummeled a Power Ranger on the love seat.

'You're responsible,' said Estée. 'You forced me.'

'Damn right Esty. You were turning into a cavewoman. If things keep on going like this, we institutionalize the little shit when he turns one,' said Pete.

'Forget it.'

'All I'm saying,' said Pete, 'is you have to operate from a power position. It's extortion Esty. This is the tip of the iceberg. You can't keep forking over money at the drop of a hat. We got a deal with these people.'

The money's not the point.'

'Yeah right,' said Pete, throwing down a shoe. He grabbed *The Power of Positive Thinking* off his nightstand and slammed the bathroom door behind him.

'Carnage in Bosnia!' hissed William, and hurled a loafer at the wall.

Caregiver Ann called later that night. If William were to continue under Debbie Does supervision, it would be

in isolation. One of the pits could be converted to a holding cell, at Magnus expense, where William would
pursue his solitary pleasures behind wire mesh as the
other tots, in social interplay, cavorted a few feet away in
the boundless air. A colorful partition would conceal the
miniature penal colony from the eyes of more impres-
sionable parents. One Caregiver would be assigned to
William's pit every day, on rotation. 'Think of the
Caregiver as a bodyguard,' said Ann. Supplemental fees
would of course be levied against Kraft-Magnus trea-
suries to cover the personalized service. Estée said she
would sleep on it. She asked William what he thought of
the scheme as she put him to bed.

'Fifteen men on a dead man's chest,' he told her nonchalantly. 'Yo-ho-ho and a bottle of rum. Drink Bacardi.'

In his private enclosure, he behaved himself surpris-
ingly well. Instead of leaping and tearing at the mesh, as
Estée had feared he would, he burrowed into the foam
and disappeared, coming up into the air only when he
was thirsty. His private Caregiver's only duty was to hand
him his bottle through a latched hole in the chain link.
The only signal that life lay under the netting, when Estée
drove in to pick him up, was a ridge that rose in the
yellowing heap, a row of brimming wake. William could
be seen occasionally, the Caregivers reported, moving
diagonally in the pit, crossing from one corner to another;
for long periods he stayed humped under the foam
against the pit wall and no movement was discernible.

Despite this apparent tranquility, the Caregivers
drilled in defensive tactics. They lived in perpetual preparedness, donned sheaths of protective synthetic fabric

over their body armor, and cultivated a bunker mentality. One morning, after locking William into his cage, Estée was looking for the bathroom when she found the locker room instead. Caregivers were dressing for duty. From behind a locker she peered in at them.

'Little Bill's laying low, guffawed Caregiver Kim, wearing a name tag bearing the chipper slogan A Well-Regulated Militia. She donned a goalie mask. 'All quiet on the western front. Save the M-80s till war breaks out,' and she pulled on her combat boots. 'Iwo Jima!' she joked, and slung a cartridge belt over her shoulder, which turned out, on closer inspection, to be a coil of skipping rope.

'Hand me the Mace,' said Caregiver Ann, whose name tag now read Shall Not Be Infringed, and snapped a shin guard closed at the ankle. 'Lisa, you pack the shaving cream,' and Estée ducked back to beat a hasty retreat as they advanced.

'William, are you really okay here?' she asked him through the mesh before she left for the day.

'A generation gap in venture capital,' said William matter-of-factly. 'Durable goods tumbled $6.5 billion.'

That afternoon she slept in her dim room, curtains drawn, her alarm clock ticking steadily on the nightstand. When the alarm went off she hit the snooze button again and again. Finally, waking in a panic, she left the alarm clock to sound relentlessly to an empty snarl of sheets and ran outside. Outside on the steps she was overcome by the whiteness of day, though the sun was low on the horizon. On the practice green, aging couples in canvas sun hats stood talking and swinging their glinting putters over the grass. She had forgotten to put on her sunglasses: the sky was too bright.

Guests on the lawn watched as an old bride and groom stood facing a black-clad minister under a weeping willow tree, in front of a makeshift wooden arch covered with a trellis of daffodils. They were blotches surrounded by a nimbus, blocked into separate shapes and then, as she squinted, connected by radiant bridges of light. The drone of the minister's far-off voice was a swarming voyage of bees, rushing water.

'Honor and obey,' he said.

Someone passed her heading down the broad staircase, a man with no mass, a blurred knife of shadow in her peripheral vision, unrecognizable.

'Are you the responsible party?' he asked.

'No,' she said. 'No. I am not.'

She left the crowds behind, walked to the van, and sat down in the driver's seat, dizzy. Her vision was clouded, but she was only half blind. She could make reparations. She turned the key in the ignition and struck out for Debbie Does.

She was too late.

The door to the day care center stood open; two windows were broken. She crunched their glass underfoot as she entered. Lights were off. Silence. The smell of rotten eggs: sulfur. She began to jog, past the crayon drawings of sheep and clouds, coatracks and rows of Buster Brown shoes, past the water fountain and the lockers, until she got to the rec room.

It had been robbed of its fluorescent wattage, though light filtered in through the high, small windows, gray beams in the blue dark. Chaotic remains of foul play — dismembered Dinos, strips of padding, torn toddler rompers — were strewn across the carpet. 'William?' she called. 'Caregiver Kim?'

Bouncy Ponies lay on their sides, wide plastic eyes staring nowhere. Ponies with long eyelashes. She stepped over hockey masks and shredded diapers. Red and green body balls, laced with shaving cream, had rolled into the pits. William's cage appeared to be intact until she noticed a toddler-sized hole in the pit wall. He'd burrowed underground, beneath the carpeting and the floorboards. There was a twin hole, smaller, in the side of the group pit. On the floor she found a can of Mace. She picked it up and shook it. Empty.

'William? William!'

She left the playroom behind her and ran through the back halls, yelling out names. The back door, like the front, stood ajar, but it was not until she tried the restroom that she saw anyone. Caregiver Kim was lying legs splayed on the tiles, her head propped against the toilet. Her mouth hung open, but her eyes were shut.

Estée knelt beside her and slapped her cheek gently. 'Wake up!' She leaned over the toilet bowl, cupped her hands, and splashed water onto the Caregiver's face. Eyeballs roaming beneath lids, flickers, and eureka. She groaned, sat up, and licked her lips with a tongue as dry as carpet. 'Where are the toddlers?' asked Estée.

Timeless elegance,' mumbled Caregiver Kim.

'What?'

'From Cartier.'

'Are you hurt? What's wrong?'

'Give the gift of good taste,' said Caregiver Kim, smiling. 'Diamonds, emeralds, aquamarines.'

'Excuse me,' said Estée. 'Be right back.'

She went out the back door, calling his name as she ran. Past a corrugated metal shed, past a puddle in which a tiny tennis shoe floated, she entered a copse flanked by parking lots. She could hear nothing but the occasional Doppler swish of cars on the highway behind her, farther and farther away. The trees thinned and she was in a trailer park. An olive-green mobile home on hard-packed dirt, with an awning over its door, was the first in her path. She knocked. No answer. Deserted. There was no one to help her. She could be alone on the earth, left spinning slowly, arms outstretched. William was the only company she'd ever kept. He was the product of a long line of bad genes, but beggars could not choose.

'William?'

A warbling sigh, close to the ground.

'William!' She got down on hands and knees. In the shadows under the mobile home something moved. 'Is that you?'

It was Caregiver Ann, in a fetal position.

'Come out,' said Estée. 'Help me find them!'

'Mitsubishi,' whispered Caregiver Ann in dreamy tones. 'Affordability, luxury—'

'Oh shut up,' said Estée, and stood.

Cars were parked outside Debbie Does; frantic parents milled around the wreckage of the rec room. The lights were on again. Two mothers were attempting to communicate with Caregiver Kim, who was lying on her back on a gym mat.

'What happened? Where are the kids?' asked Douglas's mother, and jabbed the Caregiver on the shoulder.

'For the man who has everything,' said Kim eagerly.

'That woman is crazy. What the hell happened here?' asked a bull-faced father. 'Where the fuck is my kid?'

Estée shook her head and pushed past him. From the Caregiving office she called Pete Magnus and told him to bring a search party. While she was talking she noticed color glinting on the floor beneath the desk and leaned down to pick it up: Minnie Mouse. In the rec room, Caregiver Kim was repeating her urgent message.

'Polo. By Ralph Lauren.'

Estée moved through the throng to kneel beside the Caregiver and patted her arm. 'She's in shock.'

'For the man who has everything,' mused Kim. 'But still wants more.'

'Jesus, this woman is crazy,' said the bull man to his wife. 'Marilyn, Christ, I can't believe you left Pammie with people like that. She's on something. These people are clearly drug users. Did someone call the cops?'

'My husband is coming with a search party,' said Estée. The path of least resistance lay in soothing, rote responses. Pete was used to playacting spouse for the guests. 'We'll find them. If we call the police, the day care center could have its license revoked. Do you want that?' She couldn't let the cops collar Little Bill.

'Shit yeah,' opined the bull man.

'I think we should wait, Junior,' said his wife. 'They could sue us or something. This way *we* can sue *them*.'

'It won't take the boys long to get here,' said Estée.

She located a Mr. Coffee on a file cabinet in the office, with a can of Folgers beside it. The parents stood around sipping, the bull man gibbering into a cellular phone as he paced around the playroom. Caregiver Kim was ignored: parents clustered near the front door, leaving her alone.

'Personally,' whispered Douglas's mother to Estée, tipping nondairy creamer into her cup, 'I was looking for a new service anyway. No offense, but my Dougie isn't as dysfunctional as the other little ones.'

'Oh?'' said Estée.

'On *my* family tree,' she confided, 'there are two senators and an admiral.'

Estée was brewing the third pot of coffee when Pete stormed in with a cadre of resort employees. They carried walkie-talkies and wore windbreakers, a SWAT catering team.

'This is it Esty,' he said grimly, jaw clenched. 'We find him, put him in a straitjacket, and ship him out. I got a reception back there, I got a sit-down dinner for forty with the goddamn golf-pro sponsor, and I got the IRS on my ass.'

'It was your idea. Just go find him. There are nine other kids and their parents are waiting.'

'Danny Boy, you stick with me, the rest spread out in pairs,' ordered Pete, powered by adrenaline and officious zeal. 'Find 'em, light your flare, and bring 'em back here. That's all she wrote. We'll split up in back. Esty, you wanna sit in my car with the phone? You gotta be here when we bring our boy in. Keep you updated from my portable.'

'What's this? Judas Priest. Marilyn, take a look,' said Junior, stooping to pick up the Mace can.

'My Lord, that's Mace,' said Marilyn.

'Lady? Lady, looka this!' said Junior, and thrust it at Estée. 'Mace? It's fuckin empty. This stuff is toxic. My two-year-old was here. My little girl! What kinda sick people we dealing with?'

'Maybe they kept it for self-defense,' ventured Estée.

'Look at this, people! Mace on the floor. Child abuse. Find those people, choke it out of 'em. Goddamn Mace!' He turned to Caregiver Kim, crumpling the can in his fist. 'Lady, I got a bone to pick with you.'

'I'll be in the car,' said Estée. 'Keeping tabs on the search.'

She found a pack of Pete's cigarettes in the glove compartment and smoked one with the window rolled down. Thank-you time was over. Caregivers scattered to the winds. Behind her she always left deserts or ghost towns, scorched earth and empty buildings. Bill and Betty lay somewhere under the sun. Alive or not alive. The telephone was silent. Her presence anywhere was tenuous; she was hardly felt. She was a husk of elements, air, water, surrounded by solid objects. Substance willed itself into motion. In the dark, the whites of Bambi's eyes were visible. In the distance, she could make out a pinprick on the skin of the night. First it was red, and then it shifted lower and was green instead. Finally an orange flower bloomed above her near Orion and she got out of the car.

Inside the parents had turned into a lynch mob. They were crowded around Caregiver Kim, hurling insults.

'If my kid was traumatized by this crap I'm gonna burn your fuckin house down,' said Junior.

'Junior,' said Marilyn, 'don't hit her. She'll sue.'

'It's not her fault,' said Estée. 'Talk to management.'

'Management? They're gone forever. You think they'd stick around to face charges? Whose side are you on anyway?' asked the bull man. 'This kind of crap is the disease of society! Didn't you read about those faggot priests?'

'We're all tired,' said Estée. 'They sent the flare up. Everything's going to be fine.'

'Pammie!' shrieked Marilyn, and ran to the door. Glassy-eyed infants were borne in on the arms of Pete Magnus's victorious army. Parents surged and crowed as Estée scanned the throng for William. Pete, bringing up the rear with his sidekick, Daniel, was covered in mud.

'Little Bill made a fast escape, Esty. Too fast for me. Jesus, what a scene.'

'What do you mean got away? Got away?'

'Found 'em in someone's backyard, other side of that trailer park. Eating the face off a cat. I go, Danny Boy, you can tell they been hangin out with my son.'

'What do you mean he got away?'

Kid runs like a rabbit Esty. Had our hands full with the others. Danny puked. Guy's an animal lover. It's like mass hypnotism. I'm thinkin Kool-Aid, Guyana. Luckily they were out of it. Zombie kids. Night of the Living Dead.'

'Where, Pete? Where was it?'

'Don't be crazy Esty, there's a hurricane watch out. Find him in the morning. Calm down Esty. Just chill.'

'Tell me where, Pete. Now. I'll go alone.'

'Excuse me,' said Douglas's mother to Pete, touching his hand. 'I just want to thank you! Douglas, say thank you to the man.' She lifted him up by the armpits. He hung like a sack.

'Dank oo ban,' recited Douglas, monotone.

'Yeah yeah lady. Your kid eats pets. You're not going out there Esty. I mean it.'

'He's my baby, you idiot,' she said, and grabbed his flashlight.

It was raining. Past the trailer park, she walked over a soft hill overgrown with kudzu beside an access road, scoping with her beam. The terrain grew marshy and she had to find her footing carefully on a rise beside a long ditch full of stagnant water. Rain patterned it with pockmarks under her spotlight and she counted three crushed Diet Sprite cans and an old sock. Cresting the hill she saw a frame house with a basketball hoop in the driveway. She stalked through the backyard. The corpse of a tabby cat was twisted under a bush.

Soaked, shivering, legs aching, she tried different paths from the backyard, over sagging fences and piles of tires, reciting old catechisms to keep herself alert. 'Nonmigratory tropical lepidoptera of dry forests spend the dry season in riparian forests in a state of reproductive diapause,' she repeated, kicking over the handle of a rusty shovel. 'Saturniids, royal moths. Sphingids, hawkmoths.' A cobweb stretched over her lips as she ducked to avoid a thorny branch. She felt the water seep through her shoes, felt the soles of her feet grow spongy.

Her digital watch read 10:32 when she caught sight of him lying at the edge of a mangrove swamp in a foot of water, his face above the surface. His hands were tied to his ankles, his mouth was stuffed with something red, and there was a bruise on his forehead. She picked him up. He was inert, his skin cold and slick. She removed the gag. It was a tie patterned with gold script initials: PM.

Blue-faced, in repose, he was a hideous angel. She sat down with his body in her lap and performed CPR, hair matted to her scalp beneath the lightning. Finally he coughed up water, shuddered, hiccuped, and blinked.

'William!' she cried, and wrapped him in her jacket. 'Pete did this to you. With that bastard Daniel. It was two against one, wasn't it William. Unfair odds.'

'Tale of neglect in New Jersey,' rasped William. 'Deadbeat dads.'

She lifted him off the mound, held him close to her chest, and made the long trek back to the parking lot. The Debbie Does premises were dark, though one floodlight cast the gravel back lot into white relief. She noticed, for the first time, a mound of Day-Glo green under a fringe of lilac bushes at the gravel's edge, and walked over to it with William, a soggy weight against her stomach, limp and soft, snoring. It was the last of the Bouncy Ponies, eviscerated on its side in the grass.

As she drove home, William gurgled and burped in his sleep. Bye baby bunting, Papa's gone a-hunting. Better late than never. She knew what to do.

She locked William in his bedroom and trucked to a twenty-four-hour food mart, where she bought frozen dinners, milk, fruit, vegetables, diapers, twelve-packs of beer, and Pete Magnus's favorite snack: tortilla chips and salsa. She bought in volume. She had five cartloads by the time she was finished, which the lone late-night bagger helped her push out to the van.

At 2:00 A.M. she pulled into the service entrance and unloaded the groceries laboriously. She carried them up to one of the fourth-floor suites, at the back of the building. Its window was small; it was unbooked for three weeks. She packed the perishables into the refrigerator, lined the shelves in the kitchen with cans, cartons, and bottles, and packed diaper boxes and toilet paper into the cabinets beneath the sink.

Sleep was difficult. She lay down on a couch and stared at the ceiling until morning, when she called a locksmith, a handyman, and a bricklayer from the next county. She paid them premium rates for discretion and watched while the locksmith affixed a heavy, keyed bolt to the outside of the suite door.

She was overseeing the handyman as he bricked in a window with quick-drying mortar when one of Pete's liveried doormen brought her a postcard on a tray. In the foreground were sun-bleached walls, a terrace tiled in blue, and an orange tree. In the distance was a small minaret. She flipped the card and read its printed description: Eternal Morocco. The postmark was blurred and the card was unsigned, but written in a familiar cramped hand at the bottom were four short words.

Wish you were Hear

Over dinner with the golf-pro celebrity sponsor she watched Pete across the table as he talked about the CRB index, futures, and copper prices to a new investor from Boca Raton. Instead of listening, she let her mind wander, through orange groves, past mosques and farms and over hills of scrub and sand, and everywhere was one place, Casablanca, California, the sunshine state. Her father had long arms. Oceans were nothing to him.

While they drank aperitifs in the lounge, she transported a pile of Pete's clothes to the suite. She set up a potty for William and hung a Jolly Jumper from the ceiling; on a dolly she rolled in his artificial tree. She would provide every amenity. She checked the air conditioning and the heating, the plumbing and the lights. Last she disconnected the phone and removed the jack from the wall. All the suites were soundproofed.

She went for William first. Lying curled in his crib, with only the orange glow of his night light illuminating his hirsute cranium above the bundle of flannel sheets and shredded cotton, he was not asleep.

'William,' she said, bending over the bars, 'come here.'

She bathed him, washed his face with Baby Wipes, brushed his sharp teeth over the bathroom sink, patted baby powder onto his bottom, diapered him, and suited him up in his Osh Kosh B'Gosh overalls and Buster Brown shoes. He would strip it all off in no time, but for the short trek to the fourth floor she wanted him to wear his Sunday best. 'This is what you've been waiting for, William,' she told him. 'It's all up to you now.' He gnawed busily on the bars of his crib, leaving tooth marks in the metal.

They used the service elevator. Once inside the suite he relaxed his hold on her neck, jumped down, and dashed up his fiberglass tree. She stood still a second and then turned off the lights.

'Good-bye William,' she whispered.

'Gutsy mom gets transplant,' he said softly in the dark.

She found Pete Magnus in the bar and billiard room in conversation with the golf pro, discussing a full-page, full-color endorsement of the resort that would appear in nationally distributed retirement magazines.

'Excuse me, Pete,' she said, sidling up to him with a sisterly touch to his elbow. 'There's been an electrical fire in 412, they've put it out, but it *did* cause some damage. Can I steal you away for a minute?' And the senile golfer, popping a cherry-colored Luden's cough drop into his gray flap of a mouth, nodded benignly as they coasted off, and turned back to his Manhattan.

'So you found the kid last night,' said Pete Magnus as they walked. He was checking his manicured nails, his watch, then the knot of his tie, for he was a busy man. 'Mother's instinct or something, like women's intuition.'

'Yeah, I found him,' she said. 'He's fine now.'

'Fine,' repeated Pete, nodding. 'Great, good. Where the hell was he?'

When they reached 412 she pushed the door open, ushered him in ahead of her, and flipped the light switch. You know where he was Pete,' she said. 'William, say hi to your father.'

William was on all fours at the base of the tree, poised to spring. He was still wearing his overalls.

'Murderous rampage in Toledo,' he said clearly.

As Pete stood gaping she pulled the door closed behind him, shot the bolt, and locked it with her shining key.

Stock-still, she waited for protest, for noise from beyond the paneling, through the new bricks blocking the window, but perfect security had been achieved. A grim silence reigned, broken only by the intermittent sound of mosquitoes zapping on the blue-light bug apparatus on the wall outside the room door. She hung a Do Not Disturb sign on the doorknob and stood holding on to the balcony rail to make sure, watching palm silhouettes weave back and forth against the purple sky. She had done what she could. Big Bill was beyond her reach, sitting on a porch with a view of the sea. Small consolation that each dawn and dusk he'd hear the prayers of the faithful floating by on a cool breeze to Mecca: he would never know what they were. He was insulated. It was clear to her now: Big Bill would never die.

In the lobby, she entered the names of fictitious guests into the register under 412 and extended their stay for two weeks on the database. Next she approached Maria, head of Sanitary Services, who was folding white towels in the laundry room. 'Room 412 should not be cleaned. There's a couple staying in there, special friends of Mr. Magnus, and they're on their second honeymoon. They

don't wish to be bothered *at any time.* I can't stress that
enough. They have their own supplies — just cross that
room off everyone's rounds. Does Mr. Magnus have your
personal guarantee?' Maria nodded and looked down at
her feet.

Finally she spoke to Pete's assistant manager, under-
paid and overworked, who had his rooms in the
basement. 'Pete and I and the baby are taking a trip, leaving tonight. It's an emergency. Death in the family. We'll
be away for two weeks. Pete's too busy with the funeral
arrangements to give you detailed instructions, but I'm
sure you'll do a fine job in our absence. Here's a bonus
check. I'm sorry for the short notice.'

At ten o'clock she began to pack her belongings into
the van; at midnight she checked room 412, her ear to the
door. She could hear nothing. The door did not shake
and quiver with pounding from the panicked Pete
Magnus, newly incarcerated. Still, William knew his
enemy. He had always known.

As she drove through the gates, window rolled down,
a road map in the passenger seat, she felt a pang for Little
Bill. He was a man-eater, but she loved him. Pete was the
strongest opponent he'd had; they were well matched. In
the event of a standoff they had everything they needed
for sustenance. When two weeks were up they might be
discovered, enraged but healthy, by the cleaning staff.
But it was her bet that William, when he grasped the cir-
cumstances of his confinement, would smile, blink, and
waddle toward his father with hunger glinting in his
eyes.

After that he could take care of himself. Bricks and

mortar were no obstacle to him. He was a survivalist and a hunter; he would unearth her trail eventually, no matter how old it was or how far afield, and he would find her. Until then she had, at least, the commonplace illusion that she was free.